Shakespeare on Ice

a novel by

Jake Blake

Morgan Books

Also by Jake Blake:
Sunburned: The Solar Flare that Silenced the Internet (2012)
This Too Shall Collapse (2017)

Shakespeare-On-Ice.com

Box 550, Toledo, Washington 98591

Cover design and illustrations © 2020 J. Morgan
Mezzotint of Shakespeare by Samuel Cousins, c. 1849
Image licensed by the National Portrait Gallery, London

ISBN 978-0-9858081-9-8

Invocation

Heroes appear at unexpected moments and their acts of bravery ripple through time. Many characters in this tale were real people who shaped history. I appropriate their likenesses with great respect. Numerous locations visited herein once existed, and many places still exist to this day. Other characters, places, and trivial details were invented.

I called upon all the muses for inspiration, whereupon William Shakespeare suggested I change a thing or two. Together we uncovered a scandal hidden in the missing pages of history. Time can't wash away injustice.

Dedication

Immeasurable gratitude goes to Dr. Kris Moe and staff, to my loving wife who has been my friend since childhood, and to my family, friends, and community. This book is for lovers of the works of William Shakespeare, live theater performances, Renaissance costumes, English history, and for dreamers, unsung heroes, and hopeless romantics.

Historical Timeline of Events

1509 Henry Tudor becomes King Henry VIII, marries Catherine of Aragon

1516 Mary Tudor is born

1529 Henry VIII begins English Reformation

1533 Henry VIII divorces Catherine of Aragon, marries Anne Boleyn
Elizabeth Tudor is born

1536 Henry VIII is injured in jousting tournament
Anne Boleyn executed
Henry VIII marries Jane Seymour

1537 Edward Tudor is born, Jane Seymour dies

1540 Henry VIII marries and divorces Anne of Cleves
Henry VIII marries Catherine Howard

1542 Catherine Howard executed
Henry VIII dissolves last of monasteries

1543 Henry VIII marries Catherine Parr

1547 Henry VIII dies, Edward becomes King Edward VI

1553 Edward VI dies, Mary becomes Queen Mary I

1558 Mary I dies, Elizabeth becomes Queen Elizabeth I

1564 William Shakespeare is born

1603 Elizabeth I dies, James VI of Scotland becomes King James I

1613 Globe Theater destroyed by fire

1616 William Shakespeare dies

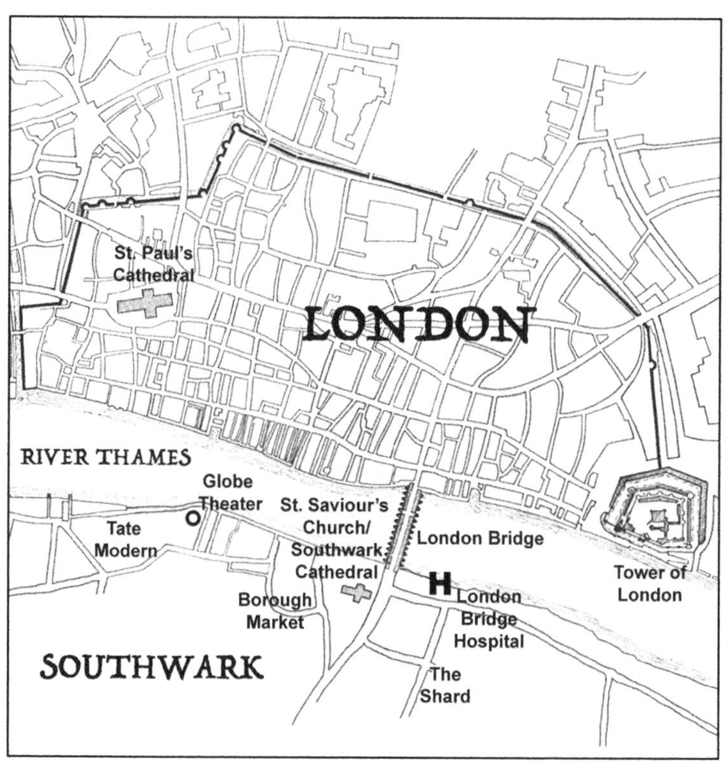
St. Paul's
Cathedral
LONDON
RIVER THAMES
Globe
Theater
Tate
Modern
St. Saviour's
Church/
Southwark
Cathedral
London Bridge
Borough
Market
London
Bridge
Hospital
Tower of
London
SOUTHWARK
The
Shard

Prologue

Providence could not find peace until the mystery of her lost Romeo was solved. It was out of character for her orange-and-white house cat to simply vanish without a trace and she worried about his welfare every day. Romeo had gone missing three months earlier and the mice had begun to grow bold in his absence.

The girl was tall for her six years of age, wore her auburn hair above her shoulders, and dressed in boy's clothing. She was naturally curious and bold – two traits she shared with her cat but not with her father, who devoted the majority of his time to studying his Bible or looking at maps of the New World.

She had searched everywhere for Romeo except for the one place she knew was impossible for a cat to enter. Late one June afternoon, Providence found herself alone in her forbidding basement, standing before an enormous oak door that was latched shut. She was holding a candlestick in her left hand but the stone walls absorbed most of the candlelight. The door's metal latch reflected the candle flame's dim flickering.

Providence had checked this basement for clues to Romeo's disappearance several times in recent months, but she had not ventured inside the cold storage room for at least a year, and never by herself. She reached out her right hand to open the metal latch and instantly jerked her hand back the moment she touched it. The door latch was as cold as ice.

Her intuition suggested some kind of evil spirit must have caused the metal to freeze in the summertime. She immediately ran upstairs to tell her father, who was always warning her with stories of witchcraft, but this time he insisted he not be disturbed and sent her away.

Providence returned to the basement door with a pair of her father's leather gloves. The gloves were too big for her hands, but with considerable effort she was able to unlatch the door and open it carefully. A sudden gust of warm air rushed past her into the room and seemed to fight against her to pull the door shut again. The ghostly gust of air disappeared just as quickly as it had come.

As she poked her head inside, Providence felt as though a witch or demon was pulling the heat from her face. She carefully brought in the candelabrum to illuminate the darkness and discovered a wintery scene from a fairy tale. White frost and ice coated the surface of the room's stone walls and everything appeared to sparkle and dance.

The largest item in the room was a sixty-four-gallon hogshead barrel filled to the brim with an icy liquid. There was a five-letter word written on the outside of the barrel in large letters that offered a clue to its purpose.

"Brine," Providence read aloud, and she was surprised to see her breath form a cloud in the cold air.

She noticed a pattern of alternating light and darkness emanating from a small vent in the ceiling on the far side. She watched for a moment and correctly reasoned the alternating pattern was caused by people walking by on the street above. She thought if Romeo could have squeezed through the room's narrow vent to the street, it was possible he came in but couldn't get back out. Even the smallest chance gave her hope. Providence searched the rest of the room and was delighted to discover a ball of orange-and-white fur curled on the floor nearby.

"Romeo?" she asked, stepping inside the frozen room for the first time. "Wherefore art thou, Romeo?"

The ball of fur at her feet did not respond.

She reached out to comfort the animal and its soft fur crackled at her touch like winter frost on a warm, spring morning. Every hair on her body stood up at once and she felt a shiver of fear pass through her.

Providence was certain that witchcraft was the cause of this phenomenon and she knew she should immediately tell her father, even though it would interrupt his studies. She decided it would be easier to take her frozen Romeo to show to her father than it would be to convince him to follow her to the basement.

With both hands still clad in leather gloves, she carefully cradled the frozen feline in her arms, grabbed the candlestick, and pushed the heavy door closed behind her.

Chapter One

The twenty-ninth of June in the year 1613 was best remembered as the day the famous Globe Theater burned to the ground during a Saturday performance of William Shakespeare's play about King Henry VIII. It was also the day the actor Jonah Henry vanished without a trace.

Jon had been obsessing over his role in rehearsals for two weeks. Once the play opened, it seemed everyone shared his fixation with Anne Boleyn. People spoke as if she had been executed recently and not eighty years earlier. Jon walked past the open doors of several empty rooms, each equally as Spartan as his, and down a flight of creaky, wooden stairs to the ground floor. He checked his reflection in a small mirror by the main entrance and overheard an argument unfolding.

"It should be a crime against humanity to kill such a sweet and noble creature," professed a young gentleman from the adjacent room. "The injustice of her death swells my heart with rage."

Jon recognized the voice of one of his friends and looked around the corner to see a group of his roommates and fellow actors sharing a breakfast of porridge. They saw him and beckoned Jon to join their discussion.

Jon wore the attire of a typical London gentleman: a padded jacket called a doublet with a stiff collar, another sleeveless jacket called a jerkin, striped breeches that covered his legs from waist to knees, off-white stockings secured at the knees by garter straps, and leather shoes.

The other actors emulated his appearance by dressing in variations of the same outfit to indicate they were gentlemen of the same social class. They worked at the Swan, the Globe, and the new Hope theaters in Southwark.

Each man's outfit was accented with monochromatic hats and capes and a thin sword called a rapier worn about the waist. Jon's dominant color was blue to distinguish him from his colleagues dressed in yellow, red, and green.

"Bearing her king a princess instead of a prince is not a capital offense," said the gentleman in green. "Yet the punishment for delivering our future queen was to take away the life of another queen: her mother. Now it makes me question everything I think I know about the Tudors."

Jon recognized the gentlemen were referring to his recent performances in a new play titled *All Is True* at the nearby Globe Theater. The play was based on the historical life of the late King Henry VIII, father of the late Queen Elizabeth I.

"Anne Boleyn was a snake with a poisonous tongue," argued the gentleman in crimson. "She bewitched Henry to separate England from the Roman Catholic Church so he would be free to divorce his queen and marry her instead. Rome wouldn't recognize his marriage to Anne and when she failed to produce a male heir, all her clever chicanery turned against her."

"You are both mistaken," Jon said. "Anne delivered a daughter and then miscarried three sons before she was beheaded. She didn't trick Henry into breaking with Rome so he could seize all the monasteries. That was all him. Pray tell, what did you think of my execution?"

Male actors portrayed female roles, as women were not allowed to be actors. Jon played the role of Anne.

"I saw it last night and forgot of you, Jon, so entirely convinced was I by your performance," said the gentleman in yellow. "I felt I was watching something beautiful be destroyed and it broke my heart. I don't know how you do it, Jon, but you did it again last night. The show was definitely worth a penny, even though I couldn't hear the final scene over the arguing."

The penultimate scene in act five portrayed the queen's farewell and execution at the Tower of London. A masked headsman raised a broadsword above the kneeling prisoner and brought it down swiftly. The disgraced queen crumpled to the stage floor.

The audience was so upset over the injustice to their former queen's mother that their disruption delayed the performance of the show's final scene. Nothing could gladden the audience and the actors had no choice but to finish the final scene over angry shouting that spilled out onto the streets and continued for hours later.

"She didn't deserve to die like a criminal," said the gentleman in green. "It made me question how people can treat each other so cruelly and yet remain so successful in other areas. Henry was charming and handsome, but he was also a tyrant. I heard he had six wives."

"I heard he was the size of three men and weighed nearly thirty stones in his later years," said the gentleman in crimson. "He was truly grotesque by the end."

"I felt like Anne was the victim the entire play," said the gentleman in yellow. "Her final words made me so sick of the injustice that I wanted to avenge her death the instant it happened. My blood boiled with anger."

"I felt she was too cunning, but also not cunning enough for the company she kept," said the gentleman in red. "Anne achieved her wildest dreams and then abruptly lost everything and plunged to the farthest depths. Yet her final words were neither angry nor hopeless."

Anne's death had also puzzled Jon both artistically and philosophically.

"It doesn't feel right to me, either," Jon admitted. "If she was so cunning, why didn't she fight the charges? Why didn't she tell everyone the cruel truth about her accuser or appeal to others to seek justice and retribution for her suffering?"

The political controversy this new play was stirring revealed an uncomfortable subject that had until now been largely avoided in public conversation.

Jon wondered how Anne must have felt on the morning of May 19, 1536, when she gave her final farewell, knowing her death was inescapable. If she wasn't terrified by death, he supposed she would be furious at being falsely convicted of treason, incest, adultery, and witchcraft. She must have known her death was necessary for her husband to marry Jane Seymour, the next queen and future mother of the late King Edward VI.

"Some people have to make a dramatic exit to prove a point," said an older gentleman as he entered the room. "It takes courage to speak truth to power."

The actors all rose to their feet when they recognized their new guest and they erupted into applause.

"William Shakespeare at your service," he said with a swooping bow that revealed his balding pate. The gentlemen reciprocated the bow.

He was shorter than Jon, had a pointy beard and mustache, and a surfeit of curly, dark-brown hair everywhere but on top. He was dressed all in black except for a plain white collar and a gold ring in his left ear.

"Master Shakespeare, we cannot stop talking about your newest play, especially the scene with Anne Boleyn's execution," said the gentleman in yellow. "We have been commending Jon's ardent performance."

"Indeed, it was," Will said. "All eyewitness accounts reported Anne appeared calm and fearless when faced with death. She professed her innocence of the charges, swore her love and fidelity to the king, and asked for prayers and mercy for her soul. Her death displayed dignity, grace, and valor befitting a true queen. And there was no rioting."

"She only did what any good mother would do," said Kate, the mistress of the house, as she began to clear the empty tea cups and bowls from the table. "Would you care for some breakfast, Master Shakespeare?"

"Thank you, no, ma'am," Will said. "Dost thou think it was a mother's instinct?"

"Aye, a mother will defend her young at any cost,"

she answered. "Speaking of cost, breakfast is a half penny. As soon as you hens finish your gossiping, I can clean up this mess."

"Thank you for your womanly advice as always, Mistress Kate," Jon said as the other actors paid in silver half-penny coins. "I did not have breakfast."

"Gentlemen, I need to steal Jon for a while," Will said. "I hope to see you again at tonight's performance."

Will and Jon left the safety of the dormitory and stepped out into the street toward their imminent danger.

The morning street was already teeming with pedestrian traffic. Horses pulled carriages filled with riders and workers pushed hand carts filled with goods to sell at the market.

Borough Street was wider than most roads on account of its terminus with London's only bridge. Crossing the river Thames into the walled city of London meant higher prices and stricter regulations. The cobblestone street continued south through town and into the green farmlands and countryside in the distance. Most of the buildings lining the street were medieval stone manors or multi-story townhouses with timber frames, walls made of lath and plaster, and thatched roofs with gables.

Jon smelled a sweet berry pie cooling on a window, and a few steps later he smelled a pile of garbage and raw sewage that was so revolting he never wanted to eat again.

Just up the street, a large hogshead container filled with frozen brine was being moved from the basement of a nearby home. Four workers wearing leather gloves labored to load the ice-cold, sixty-four-gallon vessel onto a cart pulled by a young and powerful horse. The beast of burden's lack of experience was more than compensated by its strength in the eyes of its owner, who kept a careful watch on the horse's sometimes erratic behavior.

"I love stirring up old scandals," Will said. "What are your friends saying?"

"That Anne seduced a married man and wrecked not only his marriage but a royal alliance with the Roman Catholic Church," Jon said.

"These real events were the catalyst for tremendous social changes that reshaped the world," Will said. "Henry was fixated on having a legitimate male heir at any cost."

"Is that why Henry turned his back on Anne when she produced a daughter instead of a son?" Jon asked. "Their daughter Elizabeth became one of England's greatest monarchs."

"Henry's divorce from Catherine of Aragon and his remarriage to Anne created a unique legal dilemma," Will said. "Whereas their marriage was not recognized by other European leaders, nor would be their divorce. If Henry was capable of having Anne murdered on such trumped-up charges, she must have known he was capable of far worse deeds. If Anne could not save her own life, she could still try to save her innocent daughter's life."

"It was a mother's instinct," Jon said. "Anne chose to sacrifice her own life in order to save her child. She knew her last words would have to be sincere to inspire mercy rather than outrage if Elizabeth was to survive."

Up the street, a man came out of a stone and timber building to watch what he believed was a curse being lifted from his life and loaded onto a horse and cart. The man paid the driver to take the container away with no instructions on how or where to dispose of the cargo. The driver intended to deposit the load in the river to be flushed to sea with the other garbage.

"I am come hither to accuse no man," Jon began reciting, "nor to speak anything of that, whereof I am accused and condemned to die, but I pray God save the king and send him long to reign over you, for a gentler nor a more merciful prince was there never: and to me he was ever a good, a gentle and sovereign lord."

"Anne's execution was postponed twice, so she had plenty of time to choose her words," Will said. "You have to speak as if your child's life, your immortal soul, and your country's future depended on it," Will insisted.

Jon tried to imagine a mother using every last bit of her strength and cunning to save her child. His heart swelled with empathy. He tried to portray Anne's final moments without a trace of malice or resentment, so as not to provoke those feelings from others.

"If any person will meddle of my cause, I require them to judge the best," Jon continued. "And thus, I take my leave of the world and of you all, and I heartily desire you all to pray for me."

The young horse's tail brushed against the new burden and its hair instantly froze to the side of the hogshead. The horse jumped forward to free its tail but it could not escape its harness. The horse panicked and bolted as fast as it could down the street toward the river with its tail firmly frozen to the heavy load. The driver and his crew were not aboard the cart, and they were helpless to stop the runaway vehicle headed directly toward Jon and Will.

Jon recited Anne's final words as if in a trance while Will followed next to him, silently matching Jon's words.

"O Lord have mercy on me, to God I commend my soul," both men said as they crossed the street together.

A strange noise and movement caught Jon's attention, and he turned to see a speeding horse and cart bearing down upon them.

Before Jon had time to think about how much he admired his friend, before he had time to remember all the great roles Will had written for him, and before Jon could contemplate how far he would go to honor their friendship, Jon had already pushed Will and himself out of danger.

The horse's trampling hooves and the cart's heavy, wooden wheels rumbled against the cobblestone street like a thunderclap rolling through a canyon. Jon heard people shouting and screaming, and he looked up to see men and women frantically jumping out of the horse's path, headed directly toward London Bridge.

The horse spotted the buildings on the bridge, and it changed course at the last moment to veer to the left of the bridge. The cart continued forward while its wheels slid sideways in the mud, then tipped over on its right side. The frozen hogshead tumbled onto the riverbank and loosened the lid, but did not spill any brine.

The three actors dressed in red, yellow, and green had observed the incident from the front parlor of the dormitory and they ran over to Jon and Will.

BRINE
JM

"That beast nearly killed you," the gentleman in red said to Jon. "We saw you and Master Shakespeare step right into its path and we all shouted, but there was nothing else we could do. And then you saved him, Jon. You're a hero! You saved Shakespeare!"

"I did not see the horse in time and would have been trampled were it not for you," Will said. "Instead, I've not a scratch on me. My gratitude is immeasurable."

"Thou scurvy-brained jackanapes will pay for thy recklessness," the gentleman in green seethed at the horse's owner and helpers chasing after the cart. "Go hang yourselves by your toes, you moldy rogues!"

"Be sick and eat thine own bile, thou cowardly dogs!" the gentlemen in yellow joined in.

"A pox of infectious pestilence upon thee!" added the gentleman in red. "Thou owest these men an apology!"

The young horse regained its composure once it had freed its frozen tail and realized it was still harnessed to the overturned cart it could no longer pull. The horse was munching on green grass by the riverbank when its furious master and three assistants arrived a minute later and out of breath.

The driver assessed the minimal damage overall and the men were able to straighten the cart and reattach it to the horse.

The driver had a more discrete place in mind downstream to dump the hogshead but this would have to suffice. He and his men lined up on one side of the hogshead, pushed together, and rolled it into the river until it began to slowly float away on its own. The men and their horse and cart were gone within minutes.

It would be the last time any of them would see the hogshead, but Jon would fatefully encounter the frozen container once again a few hours hence.

The crowd of spectators that gathered around Jon and Will after the accident grew to approximately fifty people. Their party followed them to the other side of the street.

Vendors carried their wares to designated areas of Borough Street, and began setting up their storefronts. There were wholesale grains, fruits and vegetables, cooked and raw meat, fresh bread, soups, and pies for sale. Other vendors sold fabric or new and used clothing.

One area in the center clearly stood out from the rest. A forty-foot-tall tower made of used oak hogshead barrels spiraled up from a single vendor space. The tower was hollow, transparent, and bulged out in the center.

Jon thought the structure resembled a giant egg on its side. He heard a tapping sound and searched for its source.

A man was on a ladder near the top with a hammer, tacking pieces of paper to the top area of the twisting, wooden structure.

"What art thy art?" Will asked.

"A symbol of renewal," the sculptor answered. He continued talking as he climbed down the ladder. "The Renaissance is over. It looks beautiful from the outside, but the center is rotten like an egg. There'll be another civil war, then famine, pestilence, and a cleansing fire before we see another age like this again. I have spent more than a hundred hours laboring on my monument to corruption. At dusk tonight, I will burn it for the Feast of St. Peter."

"Thou will burn it?" Jon asked. "Why?"

"We mortals were not meant to live forever and neither were our ideas or institutions," he said. "This sculpture symbolizes everything that is holding back our future: feudalistic hegemony, willful ignorance, religious persecution, systematic misogyny, and unfathomable political corruption. This midsummer bonfire symbolizes how these ideas will change in time."

"I understand your concept," Will said. "But what dost thou expect to gain from destroying thy art?"

The man raised the volume of his voice for the benefit of the burgeoning crowd. There were twice as many onlookers and more continued to join the mob.

"I invite your participation in my performance art for a more engaging, emotional experience," he said. "Please use the paper and quills provided to write down a burdensome thought or a personal memory you wish to release. It can be the name or initials of a lost loved one, a beloved pet, or an unrequited love; that ambitious project you never had time to finish; the last words you never had the chance to say before it was too late; or the words you've always wished someone would say to you. I will attach all these thoughts to my sculpture, and when I light it tonight, we will watch it burn together and let our sad thoughts float away in a gray cloud."

Will took a piece of paper, picked up a quill, dipped it in ink, and quickly scribbled out a name. He folded the paper in half and put it in a wooden bowl.

"Would you like me to write one for you?" he offered.

"Can you write 'runaway carts'?" Jon asked.

Will scribbled the words on another piece of paper. He wrote in an ornamental style called secretary hand that flowed with flourishes and copious abbreviations.

"You write like a scrivener," Jon said as he read over the paper.

"Experience is the greatest tutor," Will said.

Jon put his paper note in the wooden bowl and the sculptor took their messages up the ladder and tacked them to his wooden structure.

Most of the crowd followed Will and Jon as they continued on, but a few dozen people remained behind to write down a regretful memory they wished to forget.

Vendors who had already set up and were waiting for more foot traffic joined the crowd to see what was so interesting. The crowd included apprentices of bakers, barbers, blacksmith, carpenters, cooks, drapers, farmers, fishmongers, fletchers, glovers, haberdashers, masons, millers, skinners, smiths, wainwrights, and vintners.

A fishmonger's wife asked Will to autograph a 1608 quarto of *King Lear*, which he did happily.

"Did you really write *King Lear*, or was it somebody else who used your name?" she asked after Will returned the quarto. "Maybe Christopher Marlowe, Francis Bacon, or Edward de Vere? Prove that you wrote *King Lear*."

"Better thou hadst not been born than not to have pleased me better," Will said.

The woman looked shocked to receive such an insult until she realized Will was quoting Lear. Then her face lit up and she laughed. She was missing several teeth.

"I heard you married an older, pregnant woman when

you were eighteen," she said. "Do you ever see your wife and family, or do you just stay in the city and make money writing plays?"

"Happily, I am able to do both, but that is not your business," Will said.

"Who was the fair youth and the dark lady from your sonnets?" the woman pressed.

"They are whomever the reader needs them to be," Will said. "Their real identity is unimportant. How did it make you feel while reading it? Whom did thou picture as the fair youth or the dark lady? Was it someone you know, or someone you think I know?"

"It was someone I know," she said. "How do you do it? How do you get inside my mind?"

"I provide the words. You give them meaning."

Chapter Two

The crowd of spectators had grown into a mob of more than two hundred people by the time Jon and Will reached the doors of St. Saviour's Church.

The two friends took sanctuary inside, and the crowd followed them no further. The spacious, gothic interior was dark and quiet. The small windows provided some light, but most of the interior was lit by tallow candlelight that produced an odor of burning fat.

Jon and Will each dropped a silver penny in the parish donation box. The wooden floor panels squeaked as they walked around inside the empty church. They visited the grave marker for Will's brother Edmund Shakespeare, and they paid their respects to the other actors and theater patrons buried at the church, then took a seat in a pew near the altar. Jon fell to his knees and said a prayer of thanks.

Will picked up a leather-bound copy of the Holy Bible, and he examined it with admiration. He ran his hands over the cover and flipped through the thin pages, savoring their familiar, bookish smell. The cover page identified it was a first edition of the *King James Version*, published two years earlier in 1611.

"This book is a masterpiece," Will said. "There is a

music in the words when you read them out loud. The words almost echo through time."

Will turned to the middle of the Bible, turned a page, and began reading Psalm 46 to his friend.

"God is our refuge and strength, a very present help in trouble. Therefore will not we fear, though the earth be removed, and though the mountains be carried into the midst of the sea; though the waters thereof roar and be troubled, though the mountains shake with the swelling thereof."

Will continued to read the psalm and came to the end:

"Come, behold the works of the Lord, what desolations he hath made in the earth. He maketh wars to cease unto the end of the earth; he breaketh the bow, and cutteth the spear in sunder: he burneth the chariot in the fire. Be still, and know that I am God; I will be exalted among the heathen, I will be exalted in the earth. The Lord of hosts is with us; The God of Jacob is our refuge. Selah."

"Selah," Jon repeated. "It has a much different tone than the other psalms. We need not fear disasters like melting into the sea because we draw our strength from God? Endless wars, pestilence, fires, and floods are all forms of God's almighty power?"

"Metaphorically, yes," Will said as he placed the Bible back in the pew. "It was a miracle no one was hurt when that horse panicked. We could have been maimed or killed. Yet here we are, without a scratch. You saved us, Jon. Thank you."

"I barely remember it happening," Jon said. "There wasn't time to think. I saw the horse and reacted. You would have saved me if you had seen the horse first."

"Yet if we had been trampled we might not have survived to have this conversation," Will said. "You risked your life for me like Anne risked her life for Elizabeth. You acted on instinct without thinking of your own fate and we are still alive. How can we complain about anything after getting a second chance at life?"

"You're right, we should celebrate life and all the miracles around us while we still can, because it could all disappear in an instant," Jon said.

Will and Jon left the church and walked through Borough Market. The street south of London Bridge was filled with vendor stalls and closed to horse traffic.

"Shakespeare! To be or not to be!" yelled a bearded man in a leather doublet when he recognized the bard.

"Thank you!" Will shouted back. "King Henry VIII takes on the Roman Catholic Church for the love of a woman, tonight at the Globe Theater!"

Half a dozen people approached Will and asked for his autograph on scraps of paper. A fan asked Will to sign a very well-read copy of his epic poem *Venus and Adonis*. The paper of the quarto pamphlet was literally falling apart but Will was happy to oblige them anyway.

Fish on Saturdays was a rule that had greatly benefited England's fishmongers. Every available type of raw, dried, and cooked fish was for sale and the aromas mixed and changed with the wind.

There were rows of stalls selling vegetables from nearby farms, though most of the produce was small due to the late spring and cool temperatures. England's little ice age was good for the clothing makers, mercers, drapers, and haberdashers. Every man, woman, and child was warmly dressed in wool and linen. Clothing tended to get replaced or passed along and there was a large selection of used clothing for sale, trade, or free.

"I know this place we should go for dinner," Will said. "Their fried fish is fantastic."

Before Jon and Will could get to the restaurant, the fishmonger's wife found them again, and she brought the man with the well-read copy of *Venus and Adonis* that Will had recently signed. She took out her own copy of *King Lear* that he had signed earlier.

"If you're really William Shakespeare, why does your signature look different on these two quartos?" she asked. She held both signatures next to each other and there were differences. The woman wanted more time from Will but he had no more to give her.

"Change of plans," Will said as he continued walking. "We're going somewhere we can lose this crowd."

They arrived at a medieval stone fortress that was supporting multi-story, timber-built structures on either side. In front of them was a dark oak door with iron hinges and an iron door knocker.

"This is the Red Lion Club," Will said. "You have to be a master of your trade to qualify for membership, then you must be invited to join the club by a member. I am a member and today you are my guest."

Will opened his jerkin and removed a gold chain from a secret pocket. As he put the chain around his neck, Jon observed it bore a gold medallion that displayed the silhouette of a lion. Will reached for the iron ring on the door knocker, but he paused right before touching it and addressed Jon once more.

"Money and overpriced clothes are no substitute for character," Will said. "Most of these people inherited their wealth and they will always see you as an outsider. Don't worry about what they think and just relax and be thyself."

Will lifted the ring and knocked three times. The great door opened, and a porter attired in a vermilion doublet recognized Will and asked him to identify his guest. The porter led them inside and took their hats and cloaks. Women were not allowed inside the Red Lion Club.

Jon's jaw dropped open when he saw the ornately decorated, vaulted interior. He imagined a great oak tree could fit inside the immense, heavenly space.

In the main entrance was a large flag bearing the coat of arms of England. There were vast tapestries featuring lions and unicorns hanging in the hall, medieval paintings in gilded oak frames, and decorative wall paneling made of gilt-leather.

The parquet floors were polished, and the white ceiling was highlighted with gold foil that sparkled as it reflected the light from the room's crystal chandelier.

Most of the men in the room were dressed in fashionable doublets decorated with elegant patterns embroidered in gold thread. They all wore large gold chains and many also wore gold rings, bracelets, and gold-rimmed spectacles. Some men wore fur pelts that covered their shoulders.

Will and Jon were seated in the center of the room at

a table covered with a white linen tablecloth and half a dozen wine and water glasses. The cavernous room seemed unusually quiet, and Jon sensed everyone was watching them. Will saw an opportunity and stood up to make a quick announcement.

"*All Is True* about King Henry VIII in William Shakespeare's latest play tonight at the Globe Theatre," Will said in his stage voice, loud enough for the whole room to hear. "I play the cardinal and advisor to the king, and Jon Henry is her ladyship Anne Boleyn."

Jon stood at the mention of his name and added another fact that Will had missed.

"The curtain rises at five o'clock, and tickets will surely sell out before then," Jon said.

Will and Jon returned to their seats, and everyone in the room seemed to relax. Conversations resumed, and the waiter came over to their table with a carafe of spring water and set a basket of fresh rolls on the table.

Will glanced at the menu.

"We will have the four-course seafood special," he said to the waiter as he returned the menu.

"What are we doing here, Will?" Jon asked.

"Celebrating being alive," Will said.

"But why here?" Jon asked. "It feels like we're in the future. I've never seen anything like this."

"That sculptor was right: the Renaissance is over, and this is what's next," Will said. "You and I are about to become obsolete."

"I shouldn't eat too much before the show, or I won't fit into my dresses," Jon said, though he was famished.

"Eat as much as you want or don't want," Will said. "The food is excellent, but the main reason we're here is to be spotted by the aristocrats. Let's make this a business dinner. We'll call it advertising."

Will took out a ledger and made a notation of the date, location, and expense.

"This is where the biggest deals get made," Will said as he put away his ledger. "By deals I mean marrying daughters to business partners and building empires. I still have an unmarried daughter, you know."

The first course of fried halibut came beautifully presented on a blue platter with fire-roasted vegetables. The men said a quick prayer. Will took from the fish's back portion and tail and left the front section for Jon.

"Did you ever think you would be dining at a place like this?" Will asked. "I've been in my fair share of regal places, but I'm afraid to touch anything or make a noise."

"I think the trick is to act bored and unsatisfied like a prince who already has every toy," Jon said, and he began slouching against the soft back of the chair in a bored and unsatisfied posture. There were a dozen other young men in the room exhibiting the same posture. Jon fit right in.

Jon and Will were still picking the meat off the halibut when the waiter arrived with two plates of fire-roasted Atlantic salmon with sides of roasted asparagus and pine nuts. They continued eating and talking. The waiter opened a bottle of chilled white wine from Spain and poured it into their glasses.

"Art is like a mirror to society," Will said, and took a sip of wine. "It is our responsibility as artists to save traditions. Your imitation of the weary ruling class is so true to life you could be mistaken for one of them. In fact, you could almost pass as King Henry VIII. Have you considered auditioning for the role? I swear you would be phenomenal."

"Dick's not going to give up a role like that," Jon said.

"Dick Burbage doesn't always get the best roles," Will said. "I think Anne Boleyn is the real star of *All Is True,* and you didn't just get the part because you have the best legs. No other actor in England can play Boleyn like you. I'm serious. How long have you been acting?"

"Seventeen years," Jon said.

"You came from my hometown of Stratford-upon-Avon, did you not?" Will asked.

"Verily," Jon said. "I moved to London in ninety-six, and it's been ten years since I was there last. How old is your daughter?"

"Judith is about the same age as you," Will said. "You knew all my kids from primary school, am I correct?"

"I knew of them," Jon said. "We were in different levels but it wasn't a large school. I also knew your brother Edmund. He was a few years older than I."

"Stratford-upon-Avon is a small town," Will said. "Everyone knows what happened to your family. You can choose to leave that in the past and move on with your life. Have you ever thought about hanging up the dress on acting and retiring to the countryside?"

"Yes, when I'm your age," Jon said. "Why would I want to retire now that I'm in my prime?"

"You have played every iconic female role I've

written," Will said. "Lady Macbeth, Cleopatra, Desdemona, Viola, Ophelia, Juliet, Miranda, Katherine, Beatrice, and Rosalind, just to name a few. Each one was distinct and entirely convincing."

"I have great admiration for strong women," Jon said. "Somehow they all overcame the disadvantages of womanhood to achieve their destiny. They wouldn't let their gender get in the way of their dreams."

"It's funny how a man's opinion of young women changes when he has daughters," Will said. "Men think of women as fulfilling an established role, but for our own daughters, we want the freedom to do and be anything. Now that I'm a grandparent, I realize girls can be every bit as tough as boys and twice as cunning."

"They have to be," Jon said. "It's the cunning part that scares me. I can play a woman on stage but when I'm with a woman, I can never know for sure what she's thinking."

"You might consider putting some of that mystery into your performance tonight," Will suggested.

Another course arrived; steamed clams in a butter, garlic, and white wine sauce. The clams had steamed opened and were soaking in the sauce. Jon and Will each grabbed a clam and began to dispatch the meat from within the shells and discard the waste into the shell bucket.

"When I think about the amazing work that we do in theater, I am astonished that people will still pay to watch a pack of trained dogs attack a bull," Jon said as he pulled a clam from its shell. "Then they will pay again to watch a wild bear kill those same dogs. It's cruel and barbaric. That's not entertainment; that's torture."

"It's action and drama," Will said. "That's what people want to see. We are the dogs, Jon. It's a hard and dangerous world. Some days the dogs win and some days they don't. Most of the new plays today are derivative variations of the same classic themes: comedy, tragedy, or history. It's basically the same five stories being told over and over again through time immemorial. Nothing is original. I think I was born a century too late, for it seems the greatest works of the Renaissance have already come to pass. I'll never be as great as Ovid or Chaucer or Plutarch; I'm just another hack rewriting the classics with a modern twist."

Will's large forehead was furrowed in frustration.

"I think great art is timeless and can resonate for generations," Jon said. "Your *Romeo and Juliet* fills the theater whenever we perform it, and it's been popular for almost twenty years. The characters are archetypes for star-crossed lovers everywhere. They could still be performing your plays in a hundred years."

"I doubt that long," Will said. The furrow disappeared and his forehead was smooth again. "For everything there is a season. The English language is growing, vowel sounds are changing, and some day people will not understand my rhymes and puns. How will primary schools teach Latin if the vowels change?"

They had just finished the last two clams when the waiter brought a platter of fresh, raw oysters on the half shell. Both men began eating the raw oysters.

"Our job as artists is not only to entertain but to give the audience the experience of being alive," Will said. "I want the audience to imagine they are living in other places at other times, so they can experience life and see the world in two hours without leaving the room. A good play stays in your mind for several days after you see it. A great play teaches us about life and death, true love, jealousy, loyalty, betrayal, and sacrifice. You never forget it. Its characters become our friends and enemies, and if you're lucky, you can see yourself in a character and recognize your own mistakes and shortcomings."

Will finished the oysters, and the waiter promptly exchanged the empty platter for two tart pastries topped with fresh fruit. He also left their bill.

"I don't think I could eat another bite," Jon said.

"They saved the best for last," Will said. "Sometimes you don't recognize a great meal until you get to the end. Some great stories are that way, too. The ending changes everything."

Will took a bite of fruit tart, closed his eyes, and savored the flavor.

"Sweet and tart," Will said. "Perfect."

He finished the pastry and chased it with a sip of wine. Jon left his tart on the plate.

Will reached for his purse and paid with a single gold crown with the image of King James I on the front and the coat of arms on the back.

Jon sensed everyone was watching them leave as they crossed the great room to the front door.

"Being rich can get expensive," Will said after they had exited onto the sidewalk through the same door they had entered. "Money stretches a lot farther in Stratford-upon-Avon than here because I don't have to continually demonstrate my social status."

"Dressing like a gentleman shows people I have respect for myself and for them," Jon said. "I'm not playing a part when I'm offstage. I think nice clothing makes a good first impression."

"First impressions can be emotionally deep and lasting," Will said. "They can also turn out to be wrong. Appearances can be deceiving. Strangers will always see what they want to see but true friends won't care how you're dressed once they know your real character."

Hundreds of theater patrons were waiting outside as they approached the Globe Theatre. The three-story, cylindrical building towered over the nearby structures and had blank white walls but for a row of narrow windows across the middle. A red flag waved from the top turret, indicating a play would soon be performed.

"It's wonderful to see so many young people interested in their history and culture," Will said as they walked around the building's curved exterior to the back door used by the actors and stage hands. The door was unlocked, and they went inside.

Chapter Three

The Globe Theatre was more than a workplace and a second home to Jon. The Globe was a theater of imagination and creativity like nowhere else and its reputation was entirely due to the superior quality of the writing, acting, costumes, and scenery. They were the King's Men, and no expense was spared.

The building's circular interior could be transformed into any environment at a mere suggestion. Empty or at capacity, the Globe was Jon's refuge and his favorite place to be in the whole world.

When Jon entered the backstage area, the actors were already getting into their costumes and makeup. The theater's backstage was small and tightly packed with chests of costumes and props.

As he did not go onstage until the fourth scene, Jon had time to help the other actors get ready. He checked on the herd of young boys dressed as his fellow ladies of the court. They were all the same age as Jon when he began acting, and Jon realized he had been acting for longer than any of them had been alive.

Jon was singled out by a talent scout at thirteen and sent to perform in an all-boys theater company in London, where he continued to shine in a variety of roles. Before he knew what was happening, Jon landed a minor role in the play *Julius Caesar* at the new Globe Theatre.

He did so well he was promoted to a larger role in the Globe's next play, *As You Like It.* By the end of his first year of acting, Jon found himself performing before Queen Elizabeth I at Whitehall Palace as Viola in the play *Twelfth Night.*

The idea that he had been portraying young women for a generation made Jon feel old. He looked at his reflection in a small looking glass affixed to the wall, a gift from their benefactor, King James I. Jon thought his own face was still youthful and handsome. He was in great shape physically, and he could still out-sing, out-dance, and out-act any of those younger boys.

Jon began to undress to change into his costume. He removed his cap, cape, and sleeveless jerkin. Jon unbuttoned and removed his blue doublet and then took off his shoes and outer breeches. Next, he unbuckled and removed his leather girdle. He untied the drawstring on his undershirt and pulled it over his head to reveal his hairless, slim torso. Jon put on a white petticoat with a frilly, lace collar and then he pulled on a rigid, white bodice over the blouse. The corset was tight and flat across his chest, and narrow around the waist.

Jon needed to tighten his corset, but no one was available to help.

"Have we started yet? Am I late?" the actor Richard Burbage joked as he entered the backstage from the street. "Hi, Jon," Richard said as he removed his hat and cloak.

Richard was co-owner of the Globe with his older brother Cuthbert, and he wore the clothes of a wealthy merchant.

"Hi, Dick. You're just in time," Jon said. "Could you please lend me a hand with my bodice?"

Jon drew in a deep breath as Richard tightened his corset strings and tied them in the back. The corset was so tight, Jon felt he was being slowly suffocated and thought he might lose consciousness before it was removed.

"Thanks," Jon said breathlessly.

Richard unbuttoned and removed his own jerkin and doublet and hung them on a coat rack with his hat and cloak. He wore a beard fashioned to look like Henry VIII.

Jon tied a hooped farthingale around his waist to give his body an hourglass figure, then reached for the first of four beautiful dresses his character would wear over the course of the play.

The first dress was Jon's personal favorite. It was an exquisite example of the Tudor Renaissance style, handmade of scarlet velvet and crimson satin, and it was accented with gold brocade.

The dress was worn by the ladies of the royal court, possibly by Anne Boleyn herself, and it was still in fine condition for being more than eighty years old. This priceless garment and most of the other costumes were genuine articles on loan from the king. Jon knew these costumes added an authenticity and realism to the performances that attracted greater audiences.

He loved the idea that Anne had once worn this very dress, but he had no idea it was far more valuable than any other costume, even the Globe Theater itself.

Jon pulled the dress over his corset and farthingale by himself but he needed help again, before Richard put on the Henry VIII doublet.

"Do me a favor and cinch up my backsides," Jon said in a woman's low, contralto voice.

Richard stood behind Jon again and adjusted the fastenings in the back of the dress, then he adjusted the dress fabric to spread it smoothly over the corset and farthingale in the back where Jon couldn't reach.

"Who but a man would design a beautiful dress that the wearer can't put on or take off without assistance?" Jon continued in his character's voice. "And not one pocket, either! Most men will never know a woman's labor to please his eyes."

"Anything else, your majesty?" Richard asked.

"Thank you, sire," Jon said. "Don't forget to wear your codpiece."

Richard continued to get dressed in long, white leggings while Jon applied an oily, ivory-colored paint made of bone powder to his own face and neck.

A somber-faced gentleman in his mid-thirties entered the backstage and sat on the floor in a corner. He looked weak and his face was the same pale color as Jon's paint.

"Are you okay, Fletch?" Jon asked. "It's not like you to get stage fright."

"It is not of the stage that I'm frightened," the actor and playwright John Fletcher answered. "Our new history almost caused a riot on its first two nights, and I'm afraid if a riot happens tonight it will spell the end of the Globe. His highness will not allow such a disruption."

"It won't cause a riot," Will said as he joined the conversation. Will was costumed as Cardinal Wolsey in a genuine cardinal's scarlet cassock. "I heard Jon rehearse Anne Boleyn's farewell speech this morning and it was perfect. It was elegant and spellbinding."

"Thank you, Will," Jon said. "Your good opinion gives me confidence."

"It's still too risky," Fletcher said as he labored to find the right words. "I think we should cut Boleyn's farewell and execution from the end of the play and go straight to the final scene with the newborn Elizabeth."

Fletcher's physical discomfort was immediately relieved after he spoke the words and the color began to return to his face.

"Absolutely not," Will said. "*All Is True* is a sensation because it's controversial, and you never change the ending of a sensational hit on its first weekend. Removing that scene would cut the head off the whole play. It would dishonor our nation's history, and assault the memory of a noble woman with a noble heart."

"What do you think, Jon?" Fletcher asked. "Does it make sense to have a play end with a wedding, an execution, and a party for a toddler? If you remove the beheading, it's a comedy."

"*All Is True*," Will said again. "It's a history, not a comedy. Henry VIII treated Anne Boleyn terribly, along with most of those who served him. Her execution was upsetting and it makes people uncomfortable, but Henry's ambitions came with a body count. If we're changing things, let's have a swordfight break out between the king and the cardinal, or have Catherine and Anne fight for Henry's love. But because those things didn't really happen, we'll have to change the name of the play to *Mostly True*."

Richard laughed at Will's joke as he put on his kingly doublet with the extra-wide shoulders.

"I know and respect your opinion," Fletcher said to Will. "I was asking Jon."

"I still want to do the scene," Jon said. "I have been thinking about it all day, and I believe her speech is an example of humanity at its finest. The way Henry treated Anne tells of his character, and the way Anne faced her own death with bravery and sacrifice tells of her character. Removing the scene softens the sharp edges of history."

"It does more than soften sharp edges," Will argued. "If you change the past to suit the needs of the present, you willingly open the door to lies and tyranny, and you make it impossible to ever truly know yourself."

"We're not changing the past or lying about history," Fletcher said, rising to his feet again. "All I'm asking is to omit one short scene. No one wants to see a queen decapitated on stage."

"Are you guys talking about Anne Boleyn's execution in act five?" asked the actor and playwright Ben Jonson as he entered the room. "I had a great idea last night that we could use the trap door and a dummy, but we'd have to rehearse it backstage."

"Fletch wants to skip the scene," Will said.

"Skip it? Why?" Ben asked.

"I think it's too upsetting to watch a noble queen be

executed on false charges," Fletcher said. "What was your idea, Ben, out of curiosity?"

"Jon gives his speech, kneels above the trap door, and I place a starched shawl over his back in preparation," Ben said, and showed everyone the rigid headpiece. "Jon slips out through the trap door and a kneeling dummy replaces him on stage just before my character beheads the dummy. The sword falls, and WHACK! Trust me, a wooden head hitting the stage sounds very realistic if the mood is right."

"Are you mad?" Fletcher asked. "The audience will tear this theater to the ground!"

"We want to prevent a riot, not start one," Richard said. "A simulated beheading would be in poor taste."

"In a different play, Ben, it could be brilliant," Will said. "But Fletch and Dick are correct that we should be more sensitive for this play. I recognize it would be in poor taste to violently execute a real queen onstage, and such a performance is not befitting of the King's Men."

"We can still do Anne's farewell speech, but we can end the scene just before the execution part," Jon said. "The audience will know she was executed, but they won't see it. We don't need any executions to be acted out in this play for the message to be delivered. Do we agree?"

"Yes, if you're confident you can perform Anne's farewell scene so it's 'elegant and spellbinding,' and won't cause a riot," Fletcher said.

"I will do my best," Jon said.

"Anne didn't cause a riot with her speech and neither will Jon," Will said. "The scene retains its historic accuracy and reveals the true character of a king and queen, without resorting to graphic violence. I think it's appropriate, and I agree to omit the execution part."

"Then we are in agreement," Jon said. "The trial scene remains, but the simulated execution is out."

"I didn't even tell you about the bursting blood packs," Ben said with disappointment. "At least I still have my cannon."

"Wait, for what use is the cannon?" Richard asked. "There were no cannons in the first two performances."

"The cannon blast is to announce the king's arrival at the cardinal's house in act one," Ben said.

"But the king is in disguise," Richard said. "Why would he announce his arrival as a king?"

"The audience will love it," Ben said. "You'll see. By the way, it's a full house. We're ready to start whenever you are. It's five now."

"Thanks, Ben," Jon said.

Jon helped Fletcher into his corset, farthingale, and golden Tudor dress for his role as Catherine of Aragon. One of the child actors styled Jon's hair in French braids. Richard continued getting dressed as Henry VIII by layering on fur coats over his wide shoulders and adding plenty of costume jewelry. He finished the look with a feathered hat and a bulging codpiece.

When all the actors with upcoming parts were ready, Will stepped onstage to make a quick announcement in character as Cardinal Wolsey. He was greeted with wild applause by the crowd. He began speaking and the cheering quieted.

"This play is two hours with no intermission," he said.

"If you need to leave, the exit is in the back the same way you came in. There is cannon fire. Enjoy the show!"

Once announcements were made, the narrator began the prologue like he was starting a marathon and setting the pace. The race was on and only fate could stop it now.

Jon was not onstage for a few more scenes so he used the time to check his appearance in the mirror. His French braids were tight. He put on a thin line of charcoal eyeliner around each eye, then he applied rouge and lipstick to accentuate his feminine features. Jon's bodice was so rigid he had to bend his legs behind him to slip on his shoes.

The first scene was over and the second scene began without a break for applause as Richard and Will went onstage speaking, followed by Fletcher a minute later.

Jon decided to take another look at his lines for the farewell scene in the fourth act. He opened a large wooden chest and pulled out a heavy leather satchel, then set the satchel on the backstage writing desk. Inside the satchel were hundreds of handwritten pages comprising about forty plays. Jon went straight to the bottom and pulled out the pages for the current play, *All Is True*. He flipped to the ending and found the penultimate scene with Anne's farewell. He removed the page and studied her controversial last words one more time in order to inspire his performance of her first words.

"I pray God save the king and send him long to reign over you, for a gentler nor a more merciful prince was there never: and to me he was ever a good, a gentle and sovereign lord. If any person will meddle of my cause, I require them to judge the best."

The second scene was over and the third scene was underway. Jon watched Ben climb the steep stairs to the second level of the tower for the upcoming cannon scene. Jon didn't understand the need for a cannon blast but he knew it would heighten the mood and make the experience unforgettable.

He thought about Anne's last words and remembered the incident with the horse that morning. Jon had almost died, but at the last moment he saved himself and his best friend. This was his second chance, and he wasn't going to waste it. Jon placed the page on top of the satchel and walked back to the mirror wondering exactly when in scene four Ben would fire the cannon.

Jon took one last look at his appearance in the looking glass. His disguise was so convincing that he didn't recognize his own reflection. He flashed himself a sly smile and loved what he saw. Here was a woman who would be a queen. He felt a rush of confidence and told himself that Anne's powerful personality and influence would forever alter the course of world history. She was the true star of *All Is True.*

The third scene was over and Jon went onstage followed by a group of child actors dressed as ladies and gentlemen of the court.

The Globe's stage floor extended into the center of the circular room and was surrounded by the audience on all sides but the back. Two massive columns rose from the corners of the stage to support a three-story tower with an overhanging roof that covered the raised stage but not the spectators standing on the pit floor. The tower and columns were decorated to look like the outside of a royal residence and concealed the backstage area. Encircling the stage were three floors of spectators packed tightly together into row after row of wooden gallery benches. The oak building had thatched roofing that ran in a ring along the crown atop the third floor. The tower roof was also covered in thatching.

Jon quickly took his place next to a handsome young lady in similar attire. The lady was portrayed by a fourteen-year-old boy. Jon pretended they were girlfriends who were nervous and sticking together.

The actors began the scene at a breakneck speed, projecting their voices loud enough for everyone to hear but driving forward at such a quick pace that one sneeze or cough from the audience could obscure a key piece of information. Three thousand pairs of eyes watched every movement; three thousand pairs of ears listened with rapt attention, hooked on every word.

Jon could clearly see hundreds of well-dressed noblemen seated in the front rows of the galleries. Instead of an audience, he imagined he really was attending a party at York Place, surrounded by noblemen. It seemed that every eye in the theater was on Anne, even though she was not speaking.

More characters arrived on stage for the scene – a Lord Chamberlin and a Lord Sands – and the gentlemen approached the two seated ladies.

"Two women placed together makes cold weather: My Lord Sands, you are one will keep them waking; Pray, sit between these ladies," said Lord Chamberlin.

The second man sat down between the ladies and addressed Anne.

"If I chance to talk a little wild, forgive me; I had it from my father."

"Was he mad, sir?" Anne asked. Hundreds of people in the audience laughed.

"O, very mad, exceeding mad, in love too: But he would bite none; just as I do now. He would kiss you twenty with a breath," Lord Sands said as he gently kissed Anne's hand.

"Well said, my lord," said Lord Chamberlin. "So, now you're fairly seated. Gentlemen, the penance lies on you if these fair ladies pass away frowning."

The audience laughed again. Will came onstage dressed as Cardinal Wolsey and welcomed the attendees to his party, then chastised the lords for not keeping the ladies entertained.

BOOM!

Everyone in the audience and all the actors onstage jumped at the unexpected cannon blast from the tower.

"W-what was that?!" Wolsey stammered.

A porter was sent to find out, and when he returned, he announced it was a noble troop of strangers, great ambassadors from foreign lands.

With royal fanfare including trumpets, lutes, and drums played by musicians on the second floor of the theater tower, Henry came in through the Globe theater's front doors wearing an ornately decorated mask and accompanied by his royal entourage.

Hundreds of theater-goers who were standing in the

pit area pushed, squeezed, and moved aside to allow the actors to walk across the floor to the stairway at the far end of the stage. Every neck in the theater stretched to watch the procession of actors shatter the fourth wall, or invisible barrier that separated performance from spectator. The masked Henry and his entourage cheered as they climbed the stairs, and the moment they were all onstage, a thousand royal subjects moved to fill the void.

Three stories above the stage opposite the tower, a small area of thatched roofing began to smolder. A scrap of paper left in the cannon prior to discharge caught fire and landed on the dry roof. At that moment, it was still possible to extinguish the hot spot with a water bucket, but all eyes were on the stage.

Wolsey invited his mysterious new guests to take their pleasures and the masked Henry appeared to be in rapture upon touching Anne's hand.

"The fairest hand I ever touched!" Henry exclaimed. "O beauty, till now I never knew thee!"

Anne smiled and began dancing with Henry as the musicians played a lively tune. Their eyes were locked together as they danced, and for a brief moment, it seemed they were the only two people in the world who mattered. All eyes were on them as they danced. The people standing in the pit began to clap in time with the music and soon others in the audience were joining the dance.

For a few minutes, three thousand spectators were transported back in time eighty years to the height of the Tudor dynasty, a hard time that by now seemed like a golden age to those present. The embroidered costumes, the authentic music, the acting, and the incredible storytelling created the ideal setting for a perfect Saturday evening fantasy. Normal class distinctions between merchants and noblemen dissolved in this atmosphere and everyone felt as equals, like they were all noblemen or members of the royal court invited to the same party.

Anne looked up at the colorful evening sky and saw black smoke and flames where they should not be. The realization that fire is very wrong woke Jon from his actor's trance, and he stopped dancing. The music and dancing continued. Jon grabbed Richard's wide shoulders and made him stop dancing.

"Dick! The roof is on fire!" Jon said. He motioned to Will to come over.

"How can we save it?" Richard asked when Will was in earshot.

Jon imagined climbing to the top of the gallery with a bucket of water he did not have and realized it would take several minutes just to fetch a bucket of water from the river, and he was wearing the wrong outfit for that job.

"It's too late," Will said. "See how quickly it's spreading? This place is a tinderbox. We have minutes, not hours. We need to get everyone out of here safely."

Jon knew Will was right and felt sick in his soul. The fire was unstoppable, and the theater was doomed.

Anne Boleyn, Henry VIII, and Cardinal Wolsey stood at the very front of the stage surrounded by the audience on three sides. The music stopped, and the king began speaking. The audience, still unaware of the growing problem upstairs, hushed to hear the actor's words.

"Ladies and gentlemen, I'm sorry to interrupt this wonderful party but we are having a technical problem," Henry announced. "For your safety, please exit through the two doors in the far back through which you came. Please remain calm and allow our friends in the upper floors to exit in turn. We are all grateful for your cooperation."

A few people began to collect their things and prepared to leave but most people didn't seem to understand the need for swift action.

"Make haste, people!" Anne shouted in a feisty voice. "You heard the king. Everybody out!"

The audience enjoyed this sporty farewell and laughed merrily. Upon standing and turning toward the exit, they noticed the fire spreading like a train around the upper thatching in two directions. A few moments later, the entire roof was on fire. Some of the people on the floor began to feel a sense of urgency and crowded for the exit.

"Be courteous and take turns," Jon encouraged the crowd in a confident, feminine voice. "No pushing please. Let's let our friends coming downstairs go ahead of us. There's still time if we move quickly."

He stood at the end of the stage and watched the flames spread beyond the thatch to the upper timbers. The dry wood crackled as it burnt and billowed out clouds of smoke. Jon recalled it took an average of about twenty minutes to clear the building after a performance. They would need to empty it in half the time.

The Globe Theatre was many things during its first thirteen years in Southwark. With a little paint and a lot of imagination, it could be transformed into royal palaces, Roman senate chambers, enchanted forests, Venetian marketplaces, battlefields, or barren wastelands. Jon realized he had done thousands of performances at the Globe over the years and his mind was flooded with memories and emotions.

Most of the top two floors of gallery seats were empty when a theater patron coming down the stairwell told Ben Jonson that her friend was still upstairs on the third floor and refused to come down. He raced up the stairs and when he reached the third-floor hallway, Ben saw a man on fire walking towards him.

"Art thou in on this fire hoax as well?" the man asked. He took a drink from a large bottle of ale. "I tell you the fire is a distraction from the real story about England's exit from Europe and the aftermath that followed. Can thou believe we are still using the Julian calendar? Insanity!"

"Thy breeches are on fire!" Ben yelled.

"Thou can see it too?" the man asked. "I thought the flames were a metaphor."

"Fire is real!" Ben yelled. "The theater is on fire! The show is over! Thou art on fire! Thou must douse thine fire before thou burnst thy flesh!"

The man looked down at his burning pants and screamed. He ran away from Ben, reached the end of the hallway, turned around, and ran towards Ben again.

"Douse thine fire, you fool!" Ben yelled.

The man poured his bottle of ale on his breeches and snuffed out the flames. The fabric was ruined but the man was not hurt.

"This ale was no better than water, anyway," the man complained as Ben escorted him down the stairs and outside to safety.

When the top two floors were emptied and Jon was confident the remaining patrons could safely exit, he focused his thoughts on saving whatever property he could. The costumes and props were by far the most valuable assets of the theater and a main attraction to theatergoers. King James I wanted his King's Men to have the best equipment, and gave them unlimited access to the royal wardrobe archives.

Jon went backstage to find the other actors hastily stuffing all the costumes and props into large trunks, mixing women's clothing with men's clothing and mixing prop weapons with the regular props. There was no time to sort things and everyone was still dressed in their costumes from scene four. Everyone except for Fletcher, who was struggling to get out of his corset. He had removed the wig and dress he wore for Catherine of Aragon, as well as the petticoat, but couldn't untie the corset strings he couldn't reach.

Jon helped Fletcher loosen and remove the corset, then returned to his actor's trunk and considered whether he had time to change out of his costume and into his regular clothes. Richard ran backstage, still dressed in his Henry VIII costume.

"The fire has spread to the tower and to the second level," Richard said. "All the patrons are out of the theater. Everyone needs to get out now. Save all you can carry!"

Richard put on his crowns and grabbed all of his

kingly costume changes on his way out the door.

Jon couldn't carry his trunk and his three other dresses in one trip. He decided his character's elaborate dresses were far more valuable and irreplaceable than any of his own belongings.

Jon carefully carried all the dresses outside in one trip and gently placed them on top of several large trunks full of costumes and props. He worried about smoke damage and thought the dresses were probably too nice to be used as theater costumes.

He turned toward the theater and saw the whole roof was on fire. He looked at the faces of the actors and theater patrons standing outside and didn't see Will.

Jon ran back inside the burning building. Will was in his writer's corner gathering all his books, notes, and his large satchel filled with thirty-seven handwritten plays. The backstage had a surreal orange glow, and the air was hot and hazy and smelled like ash. The wooden posts holding up the tower squeaked and moaned as the fire gradually weakened their integrity, and small pieces of burning debris slowly dropped from above.

"I will take the satchel," Jon shouted. "Grab whatever you can carry and follow me. We need to leave now!"

Will carried his books and notes and Jon carried the heavy leather satchel. A hot, thick smoke dropped down into the backstage, and the two friends were blinded on their way to the exit. They started coughing.

"Get down on the floor!" Will yelled. "You can see!"

Jon dropped to his knees and saw the smoke was thinner lower down. He put his chest down to the floor, and he could see Will lying on his chest a few feet ahead.

"The exit is this way! Follow me!" Will said. The two men crawled the rest of the way outside.

Sitting upon the same desk where it had been writ, the edges of a handwritten page began to wiggle and curl in the rising heat. The words on the page read:

"And thus, I take my leave of the world and of you all, and I heartily desire you all to pray for me. O Lord have mercy on me, to God I commend my soul."

One side of the page briefly glowed a pleasant orange and then quickly burst into a soft flame that rolled black across the page and erased Anne Boleyn's brave words from history.

"That's everybody!" Richard said as soon as Jon and Will exited the building carrying all the books and plays no one else thought to grab. "No one goes back inside. It's too dangerous."

The Globe's former patrons stood outside in a large semi-circle and watched the structure burn to the ground from a safe distance as though it were part of the show. Jon stood with the spectators and watched as the flames devoured his life's dream. The timber columns and posts gave way to gravity, and the central tower collapsed with a thunderous crash.

The crowd began to disburse. People either moved on to the other available evening entertainment in Southwark such as bear-baiting, drinking, gambling, and private arrangements of carnal knowledge, or they were ferried

back to London where such hedonistic activities were outlawed.

Before the fire went out, a citizen's volunteer firefighting crew arrived to help prevent the fire from spreading to the other buildings.

"I was expecting some bonfires for St. Peter's Day, but I never imagined this," the fire chief said to his volunteers. "Oh, the irony!"

The firefighters made no effort to extinguish the fire, and they joined Jon and the patrons in watching the tragic spectacle. The walls fell down after about forty-five minutes and continued to burn for another hour until there was nothing left.

Chapter Four

Jon watched as the horse and cart rode off with the theater costumes and props. He had no idea what to do next. He had no other articles of clothing besides the priceless Tudor dress he was still wearing and its matching red shoes.

He looked in disbelief at the charred and smoking ruins and remembered that just two hours earlier, he and three thousand Londoners were having a wonderful fantasy, pretending they were all members of the Tudor royal court in the sixteenth century.

Most of the reputable spectators had ferried back to London across the Thames, and the mood of that part of Southwark had changed. Jon thought he should go home.

"Jon?" called a familiar voice. Jon turned around.

"I forgot you were still in costume and almost didn't recognize you from behind," Fletcher said as he approached. Fletcher was wearing his own clothes and was no longer in costume. "There's nothing left to do here. Why don't you come join me and the other actors for a drink? I believe the occasion calls for it."

"Where are we meeting?" Jon asked.

"The Bucket of Blood," Fletcher said. "I shall be glad

to accompany you presently."

Jon agreed the gloomy pub next to the river was appropriate given the circumstances. The evening was beginning to grow dark. Patrons began emptying out of a nearby building after spending the past two hours drinking ale and watching trained dogs fight against bulls and bears.

"I want you to know it's not personal," Fletcher said to Jon as they walked.

"What's not personal?"

"Cutting Anne's execution from the play," Fletcher said. "I know it happened eighty years ago, but it still feels too fresh. The emotions are still too raw."

Two men called out from across the street.

"Hey, man! Are the lady's services for hire?"

Jon looked for the woman in question. He looked at Fletcher and realized the men were referring to him.

"Go love thyself!" Jon yelled back. The men laughed and continued walking in the opposite direction.

Jon saw smoke and flames in the distance coming from a bonfire that was previously the egg-shaped sculpture he saw earlier. As they drew closer, Jon watched the egg collapse and scatter hundreds of burning paper notes into the air. The sculptor looked disappointed.

Jon and Fletch arrived at a two-story, timber structure painted entirely in black. The pub had red-tinted, leaded glass windows in front that gave the interior a blood-red glow from the sunlight and had the reverse effect at night.

The crimson windows of the Bucket of Blood glowed like diamond-shaped demon eyes from the street outside. The street would soon be colored red for another reason.

Jon looked for Will inside and saw him at a booth in the back with the other Globe actors. The other patrons of the pub turned to get a closer look at Jon as he and Fletcher found their way through the crowded pub together. The wooden floorboards were maroon and sticky. The walls were decorated with antlers and sharpened iron tools. There was a lot of drinking, laughter, and more than one man slumped over and asleep from too much drink.

"That was one of the best audiences I have ever seen," Richard said when Jon and Fletcher joined the rest of the actors at the booth. "There was real magic at work today and it's a shame we were not able to finish."

"I felt it too," Jon said. "We were on fire tonight."

The bartender arrived carrying a platter of brown, ceramic mugs filled with ale and gave a mug to everyone.

"I want to congratulate everybody for making it through the day so far," Will said as he stood to his feet. "I almost died twice today, and my plays were nearly lost forever. I know the building is gone, but somehow it feels like it's still right here with us, whenever we think of it."

"The Globe is bigger than any one of us, and it's bigger than any building," Richard added. "We will rebuild the theater exactly as before, only it will be even better this time."

"With a tile roof," Jon added quickly.

"Here, here," the other actors cheered.

"To the new Globe," Will said as he raised his mug.

"The new Globe," the actors said in unison, and they all took drinks from their mugs.

"Everything is my fault," Ben said with a sniffle. His

face was flushed, and there were tears running into his beard. "If I had not fired that cannon, none of this would have happened."

"It wasn't your fault," Jon said. "That fire was an accident. We did everything we could to save what we could, and the only things we lost can be rebuilt."

"That's right," Fletcher agreed. "It could have been much worse. It's a miracle no one was hurt. All we need is a new venue."

"The Greek philosopher Heraclitus said the world exists in an everlasting fire of transformation," Richard said. "Elemental forces continually push against their opposites, and the result is a harmony that our limited senses can't detect."

The bartender came back to their booth with a single beverage in a black ceramic mug.

"A gift for the lady in red from the gentleman in black," the bartender said as he set the mug on the table.

Jon looked behind the bartender and made eye contact with a shady ruffian in a black hat and black cloak. The knave smiled suspiciously at Jon and took a drink from his own mug.

"A free drink?" Jon asked as he looked to Will for advice. "But why? I know him not."

"Have you no modesty, no maiden shame, no touch of bashfulness?" Will said, quoting from *A Midsummer Night's Dream* as he moved the black mug further away from Jon. Will removed his cloak and spread it over Jon's shoulders so it covered everything but Jon's head. "You need to think more like a woman when you're dressed like one. This part of town is not safe at night."

Will held the black mug to his nose and tried to guess the contents.

"This is ridiculous," Jon said as he removed Will's cloak. "I shouldn't have to cover myself up if I don't want to. I'm not helpless. Why must men be assumed gentlemen and women harlots until proven otherwise? I think men should be assumed scoundrels and women saints until proven otherwise."

"Well said! Here's to Anne Boleyn," Will said as he lifted the black mug in a toast to the martyred monarch. The other actors lifted their mugs. "May her soul rest in peace for her brave sacrifice."

Will was about to imbibe when Jon wrestled the mysterious drink out of his hand and took it back.

"If you're drinking to Anne, then it's I who should drink it," Jon said. "Besides, this drink was meant for me."

Jon examined the liquid in the dark mug. It was not frothy and had no odor, so he took a sip and immediately felt a strange, tingling sensation in his mouth, but could taste nothing.

"To Anne Boleyn, a model for all sexes," Jon said and drank the rest in one gulp. The other actors each finished their drinks.

Jon began to feel a burning heat growing from inside his chest. The heat from his stomach rose up his throat and into his mouth. He felt like his inner core was on fire from within. His head began to throb, his eyes began to water, and his nose began to drip.

"What was in that drink?" Jon asked as he grasped his

throat and began coughing.

Richard, Ben, and Fletcher quickly apprehended the fiend who had purchased the drink and dragged him back to their booth to demand an explanation.

Jon wasn't sure which was greater, his pain or anger.

"Thou art a blackguard, a whoreson, and a hater of peace!" Jon shouted. He stood up, but couldn't keep his balance and sat back down. "I have been poisoned! Thou art mine killer!"

"Drugged, not poisoned," the villain corrected. "It's called the Black Death."

"Why did thou drug a member of the King's Men?" Richard demanded. "Who is your master?"

"My sincerest apologies, sir," the human louse said to Jon in utter astonishment. "I mistook you for a woman."

"I also apologize for the confusion," the bartender said. "The Black Death is pure grain alcohol, and the strongest drink we serve. Small doses are rarely fatal, but you'll wake up with the mother of all hangovers in the morning. I have a special tonic that works as an antidote to the alcohol to reverse the effects, but it's not free."

The men coerced the rogue to pay for Jon's tonic before they dragged him out onto the street and taught the dog a lesson. A few other men in the pub went outside to watch or join in, while the loyal Will remained at the booth with Jon.

Several well-dressed women entered the pub and became friendly with the male patrons. The vigilante justice taking place in the street was good advertising in an area known for debauchery.

The bartender brought Jon the special tonic. Jon examined this second clear and odorless liquid.

"What is this?" he asked.

"It's a byproduct of making wood into paper," the bartender said. "Your elements are out of harmony, and you need to add liquid wood to quench the fire element burning inside you."

The bartender poured a small amount of the tonic into Jon's hands. Jon rubbed his hands together.

"Do you feel better yet?" Will asked.

"I know not yet, but maybe soon," Jon answered.

"For a third time today, you have saved me," Will said. "Thou art a guardian angel in disguise. I warned you there are dangers unique to women which most men can't comprehend. You must be more careful."

Jon's brain felt completely saturated and reluctant to accept another drop of information. He knew he needed to be careful because people thought he was weak and that made him a target. He tried to look tough and confident, but the room would not stop spinning.

"I'm done with this place, Jon," Will confided. "The theater life. London. All of it. Dick can rebuild the Globe but I'm retiring to Stratford-upon-Avon, where I intend to grow old and fat. You should consider coming with me. It would be our homecoming."

"I will consider it," Jon said as the other Globe actors re-entered the pub and returned to their previous places around the booth.

"That rogue was a predator, a jackal preying on the weakest and most vulnerable," said Richard, still dressed as Henry VIII. "Creatures like him should be thrown to the dogs as in the Roman days."

"We are a band of brothers," Ben said, paraphrasing *Henry V*. "Once more unto the breach, dear friends."

"Well said," Richard said. "Different Henry."

"Garlic," Jon said as he sniffed the air. "I smell garlic. It's spicy like a radish. Can anyone else smell that?"

The men all smelled the air out of obligation.

"I do smell garlic," Will said. "It's coming from you."

"Me?"

"Oh, most definitely," Will said and quickly covered his nose with his hand. The other men indicated they could smell it too.

"I didn't eat any garlic," Jon said with one hand shielding his own mouth. "Did any of you see me eat a bulb of garlic just now? Ask that bartender what the devil is going on!"

"That's normal," the bartender said after listening to Jon describe his acute halitosis. "How are you feeling?"

"Much better, actually," Jon admitted. He stood up a second time. The room was spinning because he was still extremely intoxicated but the fire burning inside him was going out. Jon sat down again. "But why do I taste garlic after rubbing the tonic on my hands?"

"The liquid-wood element equalized the fire element and transformed your pain into the earth element," the bartender said. "Earth brings forth new life, hence the garlic. It's elemental."

The bartender's medical metaphors made sense to Jon, but he was fatigued and suddenly the natural elements were compelling him to relieve himself. He pondered whether to use the toilet in the pub and decided against it.

"I think I need to go outside for a minute," Jon said.

"Shall I come with you?" Will asked.

"No, I just need to water the water," Jon said as he stood and carefully walked toward the door. "I'll be back." He didn't care that everyone in the pub was watching him.

"You may need to elevate your salt and water elements afterwards," the bartender called to Jon as he departed. Several men in the pub laughed heartily and made lewd suggestions.

The air was cool and dark outside the pub but for the crimson glow coming from the pub windows. The street was wet and slippery from the recent scuffle. Jon detected a solitary, dark figure moving in the shadows.

"Be ye man or beast, I shall meet thee not," Jon said as he staggered in the opposite direction toward an empty, darker area on the opposite side of the street.

He heard a rushing noise and as his eyes adjusted to the darkness he realized he was standing a few feet from the bank of the Thames. He found a bush by the edge of the river behind which to discreetly squat and confirmed that no one could see him, but once in position, he realized this task was much more complicated when wearing a dress, corset, and petticoat.

Jon reached under the dress and petticoat and pulled down his breeches to his ankles, then squatted behind the bush and carefully but urgently made his signature in the mud. He pulled up his breeches, but his feet were stuck in the mud mixture, which now smelled a lot like the inside of the pub. Jon began to feel lightheaded and dreamy as the alcohol became more concentrated in his bloodstream. He pulled one foot out of the mud but the shoe remained stuck. He placed his shoeless foot into the mud next to the hole where his foot had just been.

Jon tried to free his stuck shoe but lost his balance. He splashed into the river and struggled to stand up, totally drenched. His clothes felt heavy, like he was wearing a medieval suit of armor. The bank was slippery, and when he tried to step onto the shore, he fell backward a second time into the river. Jon treaded water and looked at the stars in the night sky as he tried to focus his mind on what to do next. The stars were spinning, as was everything else. He felt cold.

He could no longer touch the bottom. He couldn't feel anything and his sense of direction was gone. Everything was dark and the water stung his eyes, but after a few moments he saw a light that was defining the curved edge of something darker. Jon swam toward the light.

He was physically exhausted, cold, intoxicated, and completely alone. He saw the curved shape again and recognized it as an arch beneath London's only bridge. Jon looked up and saw lights in some of the windows of the buildings constructed on top of the massive structure that spanned the river and linked Southwark to London.

Jon saw a wooden barrel in the water ahead of him. He knew if he went under again, he wouldn't come back up. With his remaining strength and help from the current, Jon swam to the barrel.

The barrel seemed about twice as large as a normal

barrel to Jon when he grabbed onto it, and it was frozen. He kept one hand on the floating container as he swam around it and read the label on the outside. Jon thought saltwater brine was just what he needed to balance his elements.

He was able to force open the frozen top of the hogshead, and slivers of ice cracked and fell into the water as Jon slid the lid to one side.

When he looked within, Jon saw the hogshead was filled with slushy ice water. He dipped his hand into the icy liquid and expected it to hurt so much he would be forced to pull it out, but the pain from the cold was absent.

He brought out his hand slowly and tasted the salty ice on his fingers to confirm it was brine.

"This could put my body back into harmony," Jon said to himself. He recognized the frozen container from the morning – it was pulled by the horse that had nearly killed him. "This vessel was meant for me," Jon reasoned, and dipped his other hand into the frozen brine. His other hand felt cold but there was no pain.

Jon tried to climb onto the container and accidentally fell inside head-first. He struggled to turn over inside the hogshead and felt his corset crushing his ribs as he pushed his body against the walls. He felt his way up the walls to the surface and took a gasp of air.

The freezing saltwater brine pulled the heat from his body. He couldn't feel his hands, his arms, his legs, or his feet. He felt wonderful, and was no longer angry or afraid.

Jon's brain had him recall beautiful plays performed in palaces before queens and kings, telling timeless stories of great heroes and mismatched lovers. Sadly, none of these stories were about his own life. The Globe was his life. And then Jon remembered watching his whole life go up in flames and how he felt entirely helpless to stop it.

His core body temperature dropped, and his heartbeat began to slow. Jon felt the icy saltwater had extinguished the fire inside him, and he knew he should get out of the container at some point, but this wasn't a good place in the middle of the river. Jon closed his heavy eyes and slipped into unconsciousness.

The additional weight of Jon changed the equilibrium of the vessel, and the elements began to shift within. His heartrate continued to drop, and he slid lower into the brine. The hogshead began to slowly roll in the river, and the motion made the wooden lid to the container slide shut. Jon sank beneath the surface, and became suspended in the solution. His core temperature continued to drop until his heart stopped beating.

A bubble of air escaped from Jon's mouth and rose through the icy slush to the top of the container, where it lingered for a moment before it escaped to the river and ended with a silent pop at the surface. The wooden lid was frozen shut again.

The container and its frozen contents began to slowly sink and dipped below the river's surface. It continued to sink to the bottom where it rested on its side. The current gently rolled the container downstream along the riverbed until it dropped into a deeper spot on the southern bank that had been dredged the previous week. It was surrounded by dozens of wooden pillars for a new structure scheduled to be built the following week.

* * *

In a nearby home, at approximately the same time of night, a six-year-old girl with auburn hair slept fitfully in her bed. She awoke to the sound of a loud purring noise next to her face and felt a scratchy tongue licking the hair behind her left ear.

Providence giggled and squirmed as the cat purred and tickled her ear. She suddenly sat upright in her bed and looked at the orange-and-white house cat, which continued to purr and rub itself affectionately against her.

"Romeo?" she asked. "They said you were dead but here you are, all warm and snuggly."

Providence cuddled with her purring friend and smiled for the first time in months.

"I knew if I prayed hard enough and waited long enough, you would come back," she said as her cat rubbed its face against her hands. "I'm so glad you wanted to come back. I hope this isn't a dream, but if it is, it's the best dream I've had in a long time. I love you, Romeo!"

The girl and her purring cat fell asleep together, both of them unaware that time had stopped for the animal while it was frozen, and her Romeo had no memory of the past three months.

* * *

There was a wide search for Jon when he did not return home on Sunday, and the search continued throughout the following week, with no luck. No one had seen Jon after he left the Bucket of Blood on Saturday night, and foul-play was initially suspected.

It was unusual for an upstanding citizen to vanish without a trace. Those who didn't know Jon suggested he stole the priceless Tudor dress, but everyone who knew Jon vouched for his character. His friends knew Jon would have an explanation for whatever happened – if they ever saw him again.

Posters with his name and likeness were hung all over London advertising a reward for information of his whereabouts, but there were no leads. The search expanded to rural areas, which proved equally fruitless.

At the same time people were searching both shorelines for clues to Jon's disappearance, workers poured a hydraulic-setting cement mixture into the foundation for the new quayage located east of London Bridge on the southern bank. The mixture contained a high level of potash, and when it had set, Jon's frozen vessel was entombed in concrete and well-protected from temperature fluctuations.

A month after his disappearance, the search was called off, and Jon was declared missing and presumed dead. His few possessions were auctioned off, and all his debts were settled.

That winter, his theater family held an informal funeral service for Jon on the frozen Thames. Will made a special trip from Stratford-upon-Avon to deliver the eulogy. The King's Men were dressed in warm, fur hats and coats, yet the icy breeze still gave them each a shiver.

A blue doublet like Jon's was propped on the river ice as a symbol for the friend they lost and never found. King James I provided two dozen roses from the royal greenhouse for the occasion and every man held a few. They each said a prayer for their lost friend as they placed the roses on the ice to encircle the empty doublet.

"Be cheerful, sir: Our revels now are ended," Will said, quoting Prospero from *The Tempest*. "These our actors, as I foretold you, were all spirits and are melted into air, into thin air. And, like the baseless fabric of this vision, the cloud-capped towers, the great globe itself. Yea, all which it inherit, shall dissolve, and, like this insubstantial pageant faded, leave not a rack behind. We are such stuff as dreams are made of, and our little life is rounded with a sleep."

In the distance on the southern bank, a new and nearly completed Globe Theater rose from the ashes of its predecessor.

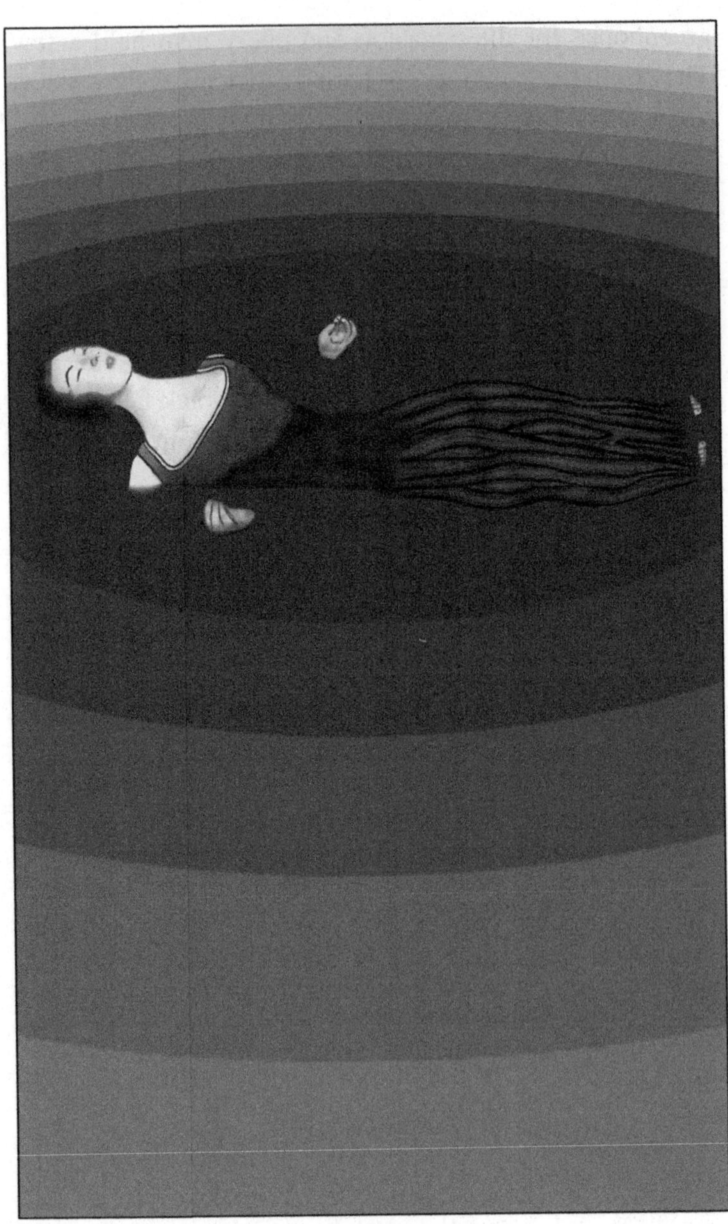

Chapter Five

The hogshead container of brine remained entombed in the concrete foundation throughout the seasons and maintained a consistent, sub-freezing temperature. The grain alcohol and the bartender's special tonic helped Jon's inner cells vitrify into a frozen glassy syrup instead of crystalizing into a solid phase. Time stopped for Jon.

The world above experienced repeating waves of plague, famine, fire, and war, as well as alternating periods of peace and prosperity.

Fifteen generations of Londoners lived, loved, worked, and died in a city that continually expanded in size from 200,000 citizens in 1613, to a population of close to nine million in the present day.

A diesel-powered river barge dredged the southern bank of the Thames on a typical evening. The barge removed the crumbling concrete foundation of an ancient quay when it unknowingly bumped into the submerged container and liberated it from its temporal prison.

The frozen vessel rose to the surface and bobbed downstream, unnoticed in the darkness. Its wooden lid had been split open by the dredger, and the temperature of the saltwater solution began to rise as the soupy, frozen brine spilled out and was replaced with warmer river water.

The chilled contents of the hogshead continued to thaw and began to shift inside. The container eventually tipped to one side, and Jon's lifeless body slid out into the water. He floated to the surface face-up, and the current carried his body onto the southern bank.

A woman was enjoying a private moment next to the river when she spotted a body by the riverbank. She saw a young maiden lying motionless in the water, costumed in an elegant, flowing dress that encircled her figure.

"What, the fair Ophelia!" she cried as she pictured the drowned heroine from *Hamlet*.

The name seemed fitting, given the Renaissance-period dress the body was wearing. The woman dialed a number on her smartphone and called for help.

She pulled the body out of the water and verified its skin was cold and had no pulse. She knew the chances of successful revival were low, but not impossible. She believed that every life was worth saving, and any chance was something.

The woman began performing cardiopulmonary resuscitation by doing a series of rapid but steady chest compressions on the body, about two compressions per second. After a minute of compressions, she pressed her mouth to its cold mouth and gave it the kiss of life. Its chest rose and then slowly fell. She detected a strong odor of garlic as she resumed chest compressions.

A crew of emergency medical technicians and paramedics rushed out of the nearby hospital with a rolling stretcher, a trauma and first-aid kit, and a defibrillator. A technician relieved the woman and continued giving steady chest compressions while the portable defibrillator charged to full power.

"Ready; stand clear!" the paramedic said, and everyone briefly moved away from the body. The paramedic placed two paddles on the chest of the patient and delivered the first in a series of shocks that miraculously started the patient's heart beating again. The patient drew in a weak breath of air and coughed.

"Ophelia lives!" the woman cried. "Hallelujah!"

The emergency workers celebrated their success.

They loaded Ophelia onto the stretcher and rolled her through the doors of the nearby London Bridge Hospital emergency room. A preliminary examination revealed the patient had severe alcohol poisoning and hypothermia. The emergency room doctor decided to keep Ophelia in a medically induced coma until her body temperature and blood-alcohol content returned to normal levels.

Lacking identification, the patient was processed into the hospital's database as an unidentified Caucasian woman in her thirties, nicknamed Ophelia for her unusual attire. A more thorough examination revealed otherwise.

It was standard hospital procedure to cut the clothes off of incoming patients with critical injuries to save time and minimize disruptive movement, but the nurse's hand froze in place as she held her scissors to the fabric's edge.

Nurse Helen had seen material and craftsmanship of this caliber once before at the British Museum. A magnificent dress was unimportant compared to the welfare of the patient, but the nurse could not bring herself to destroy the scarlet velvet and satin material with meticulous gold embroidery. This was a priceless artifact that belonged in a museum.

Helen put down her scissors. It would be more difficult to undress and examine the unconscious patient this way, but Ophelia was in no immediate danger and there was plenty of time.

She rolled Ophelia to her left side to check her dress for a zipper and found lacing instead. She cut the lacing in the back and pulled the dress up over Ophelia's head. She placed the cold, wet, and salty garment into a laundry bag.

The nurse continued her examination. Ophelia was wearing a cream-colored corset over a white blouse and an underskirt. She unfastened and removed the skirt, pulled it downwards over Ophelia's bare feet, and placed it into another laundry bag.

The corset was also laced in the back. The nurse cut the laces, removed the corset and put it into a laundry bag. She smelled garlic when their faces were close together, and she noted her observation in her report.

Ophelia was stripped down to a white blouse with lace embroidery and a pair of cream-colored trousers that tied at the waist and just below each knee. The nurse pulled the damp blouse over Ophelia's head and put it in another laundry bag. She noted her patient had a flat, hairless chest and no visible tattoos or injuries. The nurse untied the breeches and pulled them off her patient.

"Oh, Ophelia! I wasn't expecting that," she said once she had disrobed her patient. The nurse concluded her examination and dressed her patient in a blue hospital gown that tied in the back. She covered her patient with a blanket and finished writing her report.

* * *

Jon gradually awoke from a deep sleep. His mind felt like it was still hanging onto the tail of a dream that was slipping away. He became conscious of voices and other nearby noises and slowly opened his eyes.

The light was blinding at first, but gradually he could discern he was lying on a bed in a white room with a white ceiling. There was a thin, clear pipe connecting his left arm to a clear bag of liquid hanging by his bedside. He was wearing a blue shirt and his legs were under a blanket. He made eye contact with a woman sitting in a nearby chair.

"Ophelia, you're awake. I'll go get your doctor," the woman said as she left through a doorway.

A minute later, a man entered the room wearing green hospital scrubs with matching cap, shirt, and trousers. Jon noticed he had short black hair and very dark skin.

"Welcome back," the doctor said as he scribbled notes on a clipboard. "I'm Dr. Fuchsia. How are you feeling?"

"My head hurts," Jon said as he squinted his eyes. "Where am I? What happened?"

"You are in the intensive care unit of London Bridge Hospital. You're lucky to be alive," the doctor said as he began reading from Jon's chart. "You were found two days ago on the bank of the river in front of the hospital. You did not have a heartbeat when they found you, and you were resuscitated. You were unconscious when you were admitted to the hospital, and you had severe alcohol poisoning and hypothermia. You were in a coma for the past two days while your body temperature and blood-alcohol content normalized. Now you are in recovery."

"Where are my belongings?"

"Your belongings are safe, and you'll get them back when you're healthy enough to leave."

Jon tried to process this information. "Did you say I was dead?"

"You were when they found you," the doctor said. "Can you remember your name?"

"My name is Jonah Henry. Everyone calls me Jon."

"Traditional spelling of Henry?" Dr. Fuchsia asked.

"I guess," Jon said.

"When were you born, Jon?" the doctor asked, continuing the examination.

"I was born in the spring of eighty-three," Jon answered, "on St. George's Day, the twenty-third of April. What's this thing in my arm?"

"It helps to clean your blood," he said. "You were dehydrated as well."

"Did I hear the nurse call me Ophelia?"

"Yes, that's what everyone here called you when you arrived," Dr. Fuchsia said, and he put down the clipboard to tell Jon the story. "You were unconscious, you had no identification, and there was a mix-up on account of your unusual outfit."

"A mix-up?"

"You were wearing this fancy red dress and the name Ophelia seemed appropriate," Fuchsia said. "Now that we know your real name, we will call you Jon. Do you have any family members we can contact?"

"I may have relatives living in Stratford-upon-Avon, but I confess I have not been there in ages."

Dr. Fuchsia picked up his clipboard and continued to scribble notes.

"What's the last thing you can remember, Jon?"

Jon's memories were lost in a hangover fog and a splitting headache. He struggled to recall the night before.

"I was in a pub with my friends, and I left to speak with nature," Jon said. "I went outside, slipped in the mud, and fell in the river."

"You're saying it was an accident," Dr. Fuchsia said. "Have you ever had thoughts about ending your own life?"

Jon was surprised by the question.

"Deliberately? What would that accomplish? No. Absolutely not! Never."

Dr. Fuchsia looked relieved and crossed out "attempted suicide" from his notes on the clipboard.

"Is there anyone else we can contact?" he asked. "What about your friends or work colleagues?"

"Please send word to Will Shakespeare that I am all right," Jon said. "He'll know what to do."

"William Shakespeare the playwright?"

"You know him?" Jon asked.

"Not personally, but I know of him," Fuchsia said. "Are you an actor, perchance?"

"Yes, I am," Jon said. "Why do you ask?"

"You seem like the actor type," he said. "That explains a lot. Where do you work?"

"I am currently out of work," Jon said. "I was an actor at the Globe Theater until it burned down. The dress was my costume, and I didn't have time to change out of it before we went to the pub. I think you may be able to reach Will Shakespeare at the Blackfriars Theatre in London, or possibly at his home in Stratford-upon-Avon."

"I think Shakespeare could be a little difficult to reach at this point. Is there anyone else we should notify?"

"What day is it?" Jon asked. "What hour is it?"

"It's Monday morning, just after ten."

"I missed it," Jon said as he strained to get up, but he was tethered to the bed, and so tired he could barely move.

"You need to stay in bed and get some rest. As your doctor, I advise you to stop drinking alcohol from this point forward and consider making some other major lifestyle changes. If your personal habits and behaviors led you to this near-death experience, your continued survival may require you to re-examine your choices and your relationships."

"It's not what it looks like, doctor," Jon said. "I was drugged."

"Drugged?" Dr. Fuchsia resumed scribbling notes.

"I had the Black Death," Jon said. "Not the plague, thank God, but the drink. It was pure grain alcohol."

"You drank ethanol? That could blind or kill you."

"Someone gave it to me by mistake, and then the bartender gave me a tonic to balance my elements. It made the pain go away, but I could taste garlic even though I didn't come near any."

"The nurse mentioned she smelled garlic during your exam," the doctor said as he reviewed his notes. "That makes me wonder …"

The doctor scribbled more notes on his clipboard as he exited the room.

Jon sat forward in bed and looked around the room a second time. There was a potted plant next to a window on the opposite side of the room from the door. On the table next to Jon was a vase filled with a bouquet of colorful, tropical flowers Jon had never seen before. He took one to examine it closer and discovered it was an imitation made of silk fabric. He put the fake flower back and looked at the rectangular contraption next to his bedside that had moving, colored lights that danced across a dark window. The clear bag hanging by his bedside was slowly dripping liquid into the thin pipe, supposedly to clean his blood. The nurse came back in the room.

"Good morning, my name is Nurse Helen," she said. "Your chart says you prefer to be called Jon. We get patients of all types at London Bridge, including some with non-binary identifiers. We want everyone to feel comfortable here."

"Jon is fine," he said. "I'm a little confused."

"I think I understand," Helen said. "Would you care to watch some television while I remove your catheter?"

"Watch it do what?" he asked. "I'm not sure what you mean. What are you removing?"

Nurse Helen picked up a black rectangular object from the table and pressed the bumps on it while she stared at a dark window that faced Jon's bed on the opposite wall. The window flashed into a brilliant display of moving colors and noises. She pressed down on a few of the bumps and the pictures in the window changed. She handed the rectangular object to Jon.

"You can change it to whatever you want," she said.

The nurse slipped on a pair of stretchy white gloves and lifted up the blanket covering Jon's legs. He shifted uncomfortably in his bed and felt yet another unusual sensation he couldn't explain. "Now that you're awake, you don't need this anymore," she said.

Jon didn't recognize the people's faces in the magical window. Some were talking, some were shouting, and some were crying. Jon pressed the bumps on the handheld device. The window was even more annoying with the sound turned all the way up, but he didn't know how to turn it down. He kept pressing bumps and the window changed to a comedy program. People were laughing.

"This will feel a little weird," Helen said, then removed Jon's catheter.

"Why did you do that?!" Jon asked while she finished cleaning up with a damp cloth. He felt as though that part of him had been turned inside out.

"You don't need it," she repeated. "It might burn the next time you go, but it's better if you do it yourself from now on. You'll thank me later."

The moving faces on the window continued laughing, and Jon felt a flash of anger.

"Thou canst not speak of that thou dost not feel!" Jon lectured. The faces continued their mocking laugh at full volume. Jon began cursing at the window. He hated it.

Nurse Helen picked up the rectangular device and turned off the window. The room was quiet again.

"Would you care to read a newspaper instead?" Helen

asked. She kept the rectangular device.

"I suppose I will take a gander," Jon said calmly, having never heard of a newspaper before.

Nurse Helen left the room and returned with a tabloid newspaper, which she gave to Jon. The headlines made no sense to Jon. There was some kind of climate problem that was causing record-breaking heat waves, famine, drought, and flooding around the world. The polar ice caps were melting and sea levels were rising.

He turned the page, and inside was a photograph of a young woman in a two-piece bathing suit posing provocatively. Jon looked at the date printed on the top corner of the page. Not only were the day and month wrong, the year was way off. He checked the date on several pages to make sure it wasn't a mistake.

"What century is it?" Jon asked Helen.

"The twenty-first," Helen said.

"I shouldn't be here," Jon said as he stared at his feet. "I feel like I'm in the wrong place at the wrong time."

"I know what you mean," she said.

"Verily, I do not belong here. Not now."

"Everybody feels that way about the hospital, Jon," Helen said as she took away the newspaper. "You need to rest and recover your strength. We will try to get you out of bed after dinner, but for now, the best way to pass the time is to take your mind off your situation. How about a book instead? The hospital has a decent library but most of the books are old."

"How old?" Jon asked. "Do you have anything from the seventeenth century?"

"There should be a Bible in your nightstand."

Jon opened the drawer and found a leather-bound copy of the *King James Version.* He opened it to the middle and smelled the aroma of the pages.

"This is perfect," he said. "Thank you, Helen."

Jon looked down at the place where the Bible had opened and began reading Psalm 22.

"My God, my God, why hast thou forsaken me? Why art thou so far from helping me, and from the words of my roaring?"

He continued reading in silence until it was time for dinner, and a hospital worker brought him his food on a tray. It was not the best food he had ever eaten but it was wholesome and it gave him strength. He read stories of Jesus resurrecting the dead in John, Luke, and Mark, and he read about the men in Genesis who lived for more than 900 years. They brought him supper, and he went for a walk. He continued reading his Bible until dark, then put it away, turned off his light, and went to sleep.

An hour later, a hospital orderly came in to check Jon's vitals, and they had to wake him so he could swallow some pills. The hospital room door closed with a slam.

Jon went back to sleep for another two hours until a different hospital orderly came in to check his vitals. The orderly didn't try to wake him but the hospital corridors were very well lit both day and night and bright light spilled into his room whenever the door was opened. Unless the door was carefully closed like Nurse Helen did, it would slam shut every time.

Jon spent two more restless days and nights at the

hospital. He ate strange foods from sealed plastic containers. A physical rehabilitation specialist helped Jon learn to balance and walk again, go up and down steps, and made sure he could pass simple memory tests and perform common tasks like frying an egg and making instant coffee – things he had never done before.

He took long walks around the hospital wings and made small talk with the nurses and orderlies. He stared out the large windows at the river and the thriving city below, and gazed at the calming artwork hanging on the hospital walls. These were not landscapes or portraits, but Jon felt an emotional, almost primal connection with many of the paintings that surprised him.

On his last day at the hospital, the staff brought Jon his belongings, and he put on his breeches and blouse. One of the doctors donated a ridiculously large designer shopping bag with twine handles that advertised the name of a women's clothing brand. The hospital staff put the Tudor dress, bodice, and farthingale into the bag for him, and they included replacement lacing for the dress and bodice. All of his clothes had been dry cleaned and were encased in transparent plastic bags.

Jon had arrived without footwear, so the hospital provided him with a pair of rubber clogs. There were about twenty large air holes on the toe area for ventilation that made the shoes weigh next to nothing. Jon thought they looked unusual but found them to be very comfortable. Almost every nurse, orderly, or hospital staff member wore the same style of footwear.

The doctor gave Jon his discharge instructions.

"Hello, Jon," Dr. Fuchsia said. "Your condition is stable, and you're healthy enough to leave. We were unable to locate any records for you in our database or anything about you on the Internet. I'm not prescribing any medications, but I am advising you to avoid drinking alcohol. Water, tea, coffee, juice, and even non-alcoholic cocktails are easy alternatives that won't put your health at great risk. Try to eat well and get exercise. Do you have any place you can go?"

"I have myself, everything I know, and these few possessions," Jon said. "I don't know what to expect out there, but I will do my best."

"I wish you good luck and Godspeed," Fuchsia said.

"Thank you for saving my life," Jon said as he shook hands with his doctor. Jon picked up his bag of clothes and left his hospital room.

Helen and a dozen other nurses were waiting in the hallway to give Jon good wishes. Jon said goodbye and thanked each of them for choosing to help people like him.

Chapter Six

The first place Jon wanted to go was home to his apartment. He looked at a map, oriented himself with the river, and knew he needed to head southwest.

He walked around the hospital to the south side of the building so he could see where he needed to go, and that's when he first saw the colossal, inverted icicle of a building that stabbed upward out of the ground and glittered as it cut the sky. The building was so massive and its footprint was so large that Jon could see from a distance that his former home was gone.

He saw the route he needed to take and began to step into the street when he heard a loud trumpeting noise and narrowly missed being struck by a speeding carriage from his right.

Jon remembered being nearly struck by a horse a few days earlier in almost the same place, and he lambasted himself for being so careless. There were no horses pulling these carriages and they appeared to move on their own power at terrific speeds.

He waited for a break in the traffic and after a minute all the cars stopped, and a black box on the opposite side of the street displayed an image of a man walking. Jon saw a dozen other pedestrians crossing the street, and followed them to the other side. The traffic resumed.

Jon found the site of his former home. The address was correct, but instead of the two-story building with the nice lobby, it was replaced by a skyscraper called the Shard. Jon went inside the lobby and asked the porter if they had any rooms available, possibly long term.

"We have many excellent rooms available," the porter said. "I will need to see a major credit card and some identification."

The porter was tall, had a hairless face covered in freckles, blue eyes, curly orange hair, and piercings in both ears and in one nostril. They were wearing a yellow blazer jacket over a white shirt, purple trousers, and white shoes.

"I have neither at the moment," Jon said.

"Our hotel rooms start at five hundred pounds per night," the porter said, and examined Jon's unusual attire.

"Five hundred pounds? Is everyone here a wealthy merchant or nobleman?" Jon asked.

"Pretty much," the porter admitted. "This has information about our residential units and prices," the porter said and handed Jon a brochure. "You can find a lot more information on the Shard's website."

Jon looked at the other people in the lobby. They were all well-dressed, and he was not. Jon felt out of place again. He looked at the brochure. It said the Shard was the tallest building in Europe at 310 meters. Some of the residential units near the top were priced at £10 million.

"These prices are outrageous," Jon said "I could own a castle in the countryside for the cost of one unit upstairs."

"I know what you mean," the porter said, leaning forward and speaking in a confidential tone. "I couldn't afford to live in London at that price either."

"I used to live here many years ago, before all this was built," Jon said. "Maybe you can still help me. I'm looking for somewhere modest to stay. It doesn't have to be large or luxurious, but a view would be great."

"There are lots of nice hotels in this area that are much cheaper, but none of them have a view like the Shard. If you think you may need somewhere free to stay tonight, you could visit the shelter next to Southwark Cathedral."

Jon thanked the porter for the suggestion. He put the brochure in his bag and made his way to the ground level.

He followed the sidewalk with the other pedestrians around the building, and when he came to the next place he wanted to cross, Jon waited with the other pedestrians for the traffic lights to change. Nearly everyone who was waiting for a light to change was also looking down at shiny rectangular devices they held in their hands.

The lights changed, and the moving traffic stopped so those waiting could have a turn. Jon followed the flow of foot traffic across the boulevard to the cathedral on the opposite side of the street.

He was disoriented for a moment as he stood in front of the Gothic cathedral. The building was nothing like the St. Saviour's Church he remembered, and its singular tower bore a strong resemblance to the old St. Paul's Cathedral he knew on the other side of the river.

Jon wondered if he was at the right place. Every sign and map confirmed he was at Southwark Cathedral. He spent a few minutes outside admiring the cathedral's pointed arches, flying buttresses, and the stone tracery wrapped around its massive windows of stained glass.

As Jon passed through the dark oak doors, he was equally impressed by the cathedral's vaulted interior. There were few other parishioners inside. Jon said a prayer and then explored the inside of the cathedral. He admired the Gothic architecture and large pictorial glass mosaics.

Jon was surprised to find one such window decorated not with saints but with fairies and jesters, a comedy of men with horse's heads and ripened bellies. A wizard king with a white beard stood with arms outstretched from the central window, while behind him a grotesque creature crawled obediently. The third panel featured a tragic prince holding a skull surrounded by kings, queens, and knights and at the bottom, two old feeble men with nothing but their memories.

Jon recognized each of the figures as characters from the plays he had performed during his career. He knew this had to be a tribute to his friend and was so excited to tell Will about this new window that he briefly forgot his situation. Below the window was a marble effigy of a reclining bald man in a doublet, jerkin, and breeches. An inscription read, "In memory of William Shakespeare for several years an inhabitant of this parish."

Reality stabbed his heart like a dagger and the pain of it brought him to his knees. He began sweating and breathing heavily as he knelt in front of the tribute. Jon reminded himself that it was no longer the year 1613 and tried to detach himself from his emotions. A sign indicated

Shakespeare's body was buried elsewhere. Jon rose to his feet and continued exploring the interior to see if he could find Will's grave.

Jon recognized the names of more colleagues and peers, some of whom had already died when he was alive, and some who died soon afterward. He could still picture their faces and remember the sound of their voices, but somehow last week to Jon was four centuries earlier. Will was gone. Richard, Ben, and Fletcher, his friends, neighbors, and everyone Jon had ever known were dead and had been dead for so long, not even their bones remained.

He searched the rest of the interior, then went outside and searched the gravestones in the cemetery, without luck. Jon returned to the tribute window inside and studied it for clues. The figures themselves were meaningless without knowledge of their characters. Their spoken words brought them to life, and through them, an understanding of the world. There was an order to the world, and it was clear that Jon was at a disadvantage.

He was growing increasingly frustrated when a ten-year-old girl approached him and asked what was wrong.

"I'm trying to find someone's grave, and I'm not having much luck," Jon said.

"You should ask for help," the girl said. "That's what I do when I get stuck."

"Do you know where William Shakespeare is buried?" Jon asked.

"Yes, I do," she said. "William Shakespeare is buried in Stratford-upon-Avon."

“How do you know that?” Jon asked.

“I learned it in school,” the girl said proudly. “William Shakespeare was the greatest writer of all time.”

“Of all time,” Jon repeated. “That sounds unrivaled.”

“What does unrivaled mean?” the girl asked. “Why are you wearing dirty pajamas?”

“You’re right, these clothes are very old, and I should get new ones,” Jon said as he stood and collected his belongings. “Thank you for your help.”

Jon continued exploring the streets and found the shelter recommended by the porter at the Shard. It looked clean, and it was free. A sign said guests had to be sober and not make a disturbance, or they would be asked to leave. It sounded better to Jon than sleeping on the street.

He found an area near the waterfront where everyone was clean and well dressed and looked civilized. Jon attempted to enter a fine clothing store, but the doorman would not let him inside on account of his wardrobe not meeting their dress code. Jon followed the foot traffic inside a nice restaurant but was again turned away on account of being dressed like a bum.

Jon decided to lower his standards and kept walking until he found a place where most of the people were dressed like him in shorts and baggy shirts. He went in a place that advertised fast food. The interior was brightly lit and every surface was hard and polished to a shine, though he did not see anything made of wood or metal.

Jon asked for a fish sandwich, but he had no money to pay for it. The porter called their manager, and Jon felt them both scrutinize his appearance.

"People are expected to pay for food," the manager lectured Jon.

"Please, sir," Jon said. "I'm very hungry."

"Next time you come back, bring money," the manager said, and gave Jon the hot sandwich for free. "I'm running a business, not a charity."

"Thank you, sir, and God bless you," Jon said as he took his fish sandwich outside.

He sat on a bench facing the river Thames as he ate the sandwich and wondered what he would do next. He thought he should try to get a job, but he had no modern skills. Everything he had received thus far was from the kindness of strangers. He had to keep trying because the bottom was no place to be.

He felt the presence of another person standing next to him and turned around to see a figure with messy hair and soiled clothing. Jon stepped back from the wretched figure, and it stepped away from him at the same time. It took Jon a few seconds to recognize his own reflection in the street window, and he felt a swelling of shame, anger, and pity once he saw himself as others saw him.

Jon watched as hundreds of people began to exit the tall office buildings and fill the sidewalks in the rush to get home, find some supper, or meet with a friend after work. Street lights began to push out the darkness, and the night life awoke as the sun slowly sank below the horizon.

Jon stood on the sidewalk and watched the city move around him. Most people were looking straight ahead at nothing or were looking down at shiny rectangular devices in their hands. He could see them, but it was easier for people to ignore unpleasant realities. He was invisible to most of them – a ghost.

He resented being cast out of society and felt his emotions rise inside him. Shakespeare's words poured from his mouth as he knelt on the sidewalk.

"O, that this too too sullied flesh would melt, thaw and resolve itself into a dew," Jon cried out, quoting *Hamlet*. "Or that the Everlasting had not fixed his canon against self-slaughter! O God! God! How weary, stale, flat and unprofitable, seem to me all the uses of this world! Fie on it! Ah fie!"

Jon noticed several passersby had gathered to watch him perform. He finished the monologue with such heartfelt passion that people were wiping their tears and applauding when he finished. A few bystanders opened their wallets or reached into their pockets and tossed a few coins and paper bills onto the sidewalk in front of Jon.

"Shakespeare!" yelled a man from the back of the crowd. "To be or not to be!"

Jon was surprised that people recognized *Hamlet* and was happy to indulge the crowd with the famous monolog. He thought about his own near-death experiences and all of the people he had once known who were no longer.

"To be, or not to be: that is the question," he began quoting from memory. His mind was taken back to the first performance of *Hamlet* at Whitehall Palace before Elizabeth I and her guests. Jon felt Will's words and thoughts speaking through him as he continued reciting the rest of the lines from memory. Jon played the tragic nymph Ophelia but he knew all of the parts. He remembered the performance was long but quickly paced and the ending was spectacular and gruesome.

Jon finished Hamlet's introspective thoughts about over-thinking problems ad nauseam and took a gracious bow to the two dozen bystanders who had stopped to watch. They clapped and nodded in agreement. Some people smiled as they walked away and some didn't. Many people tossed money at Jon's feet, and he thanked them as he gathered their donations together. He counted the money and saw he had almost eight pounds in change.

Jon's stomach growled with hunger so he picked up his bags and retraced his steps back to the fast-food restaurant. He went inside and approached the register. The staff recognized Jon from earlier, and the manager came out to talk with him. Jon smiled and put his change on the counter in a pile.

"I came back with some money," Jon said with dignity. "This is for the food you gave me earlier and for the halibut and chips meal."

The food was nearly as fast as the service, and in hardly any time, Jon was enjoying fried halibut and chips in an empty corner of the restaurant. After he was finished eating, Jon left the restaurant and purchased some soap and a safety razor from a corner shop with his remaining money. He returned to the shelter next to the cathedral.

The inside of the shelter was a spacious room filled with about two hundred beds. The beds were surplus canvas stretched over a frame of hollow metal tubes. A volunteer gave everyone a blanket and a bottle of water. Jon found a cot and used his giant designer bag as a pillow.

He tried to make himself comfortable and told himself this was better and safer than sleeping outdoors. The empty beds were filling up with occupants, and it took some people longer to get settled than others. Jon closed his eyes and listened to the sounds of strange people talking, coughing, or snoring.

Jon awoke Friday morning at dawn and saw that every bed had been filled during the night and most of the 200 occupants were still sleeping. He collected his garment bag and had a cup of the shelter's free coffee and a piece of the last bran muffin. He washed himself in the shelter's lavatory and shaved his face in front of the large mirror. Jon studied his own reflection and decided he would try something different today.

The Tudor dress had been a liability to Jon since the fire, but it had survived intact, along with the corset and petticoat. He decided to start looking at the dress as an asset instead of a liability.

It was made from the best materials available by King Henry VIII's royal dressmakers and couturiers. Jon had convinced 3,000 spectators that he was Anne Boleyn, and he was confident he could do it again if he had to.

Jon had spent hours observing well-dressed business professionals go to work the day before. They wore suits, dresses, or suit jackets with skirts. Jon paid attention to how the women in dresses moved. They walked with poise and grace as they moved effortlessly in cute shoes with raised heels. He studied facial expressions, hair styles, and the way they moved, especially their hands.

As Jon threaded the new lacing into the back of the

corset and dress, he reminded himself that he had already been mistaken for a woman several times while wearing the dress and bad things had happened. New dangers had appeared that could have been avoided if he had been a more sensible woman and gone home.

He needed to think like a lady when he was dressed like one, and the simplest way for him to do that was to play a female character and improvise.

Jon decided he would wear the dress and pretend to be the stouthearted Anne.

"I humbly summon for the spirit of your majesty, Queen Anne, to guide my actions this day as I give your dress another tour of the city you so loved," Jon said to his reflection. "Anne Boleyn, you shall live again."

He wet and groomed his hair in front of the mirror and studied his reflection. He didn't think he looked like a woman. His undershirt was soiled so he took it off. He reached into the designer garment bag and removed the white bodice and put it on over his head. He pulled the corset into position but couldn't reach the strings in the back to tighten it.

A homeless man with unkempt hair and a bushy beard came into the lavatory and saw Jon by the mirror. The man's clothes were clean but threadbare.

"Hello, friend, could thou lend me a hand?" Jon asked the man.

"What do you need?" the man asked.

"Could you please pull these strings at the back of my bodice, tightly?" Jon asked sweetly.

"What do you need a bodice for?" the man asked as

he approached Jon cautiously.

"I'm trying to get a job," Jon said. "And I have to wear this under my clothes."

"I hate job interviews," the man said as he began to tighten the new laces on the back of Jon's corset. "I hope you get the job."

Jon held in his breath as the man tied the strings in a knot. He had lost a little weight since he last wore the corset, and it fit him better.

"A million thanks and maybe one more before you leave," Jon said. The man went to use a toilet in the bathroom stalls and latched the door shut. Jon fluffed out and fastened the hooped farthingale around his waist and clipped it to the bodice.

Next, Jon removed the dress from the plastic dry-cleaning bag and pulled it on over his head. The dress fit loosely, and he smoothed it over the corset and petticoat. The draw strings were in the back, and he couldn't reach them. He looked at his reflection again and was startled by his metamorphosis into a lady of the court. He groomed his hair, pinched his cheeks to make them pink, and flashed his reflection a wide smile.

"This is your big moment, Anne," Jon said in his character's contralto voice. "You've got this!"

A toilet flushed. The bearded man came out of the toilet stall and looked surprised to see a woman.

"Could you help me fasten the back of this dress?" Jon asked. "I promise it's the last favor I'll ask."

Jon smoothed the dress over the corset and petticoat again as the man tightened and tied the dress in the back.

"I don't know what the job is, but better you than me," the man said when he had finished.

"Thank you again, good sir," Jon said with a curtsy.

The man held the door open for Jon as he left the lavatory. Jon stepped out onto the street, and the first person who saw him complimented the beautiful dress and the woman who wore it.

Jon returned to the street with the fancy shops where there were hundreds of well-dressed professionals on their way to work. Some noticed Jon, but the rest kept walking.

"You look like you're having a shoe emergency," said a woman's voice from behind him.

Jon turned around to see who had spoken, and for a brief moment he thought it was either Anne Boleyn's ghost or his own reflection dressed as Anne. She was about the same height as Jon at five feet, seven inches and appeared to be about the same age. The woman was wearing a light blue spring dress with a floral print and a sweater that did not match. The sweater matched her blood-red, high-heeled shoes.

"I left the house thinking that this sweater was fine because it compliments my shoes, and my shoes are fine because they match my sweater, but neither one matches my dress," the woman said. "I just had this feeling that I should get different shoes that match my dress, and that's when I saw you, wearing the perfect dress for my shoes but the wrong shoes for your own dress. That's an amazing dress, by the way. What size are your feet?"

Jon wasn't sure but he slipped off his synthetic clogs and held his bare foot next to the woman's.

"We're the same size," she said. "I knew it! I was meant to meet you today. Can you accept a gift from a complete stranger? My name's Emma."

Emma extended her hand, and Jon took it gracefully.

"I'm Anne," he said, still in character. "You would be doing me a huge favor."

"If you can wait here a few minutes, I'm going to get a pair of pumps I've been dreaming of all week that just happen to match this dress," she said. "I'll be right back."

Jon felt energized the moment Emma left. He watched her walk into a nearby shoe store and noted how she moved her legs with confidence and authority.

The wooden heels of her shoes made a powerful and repetitive clacking noise against the sidewalk as Emma walked. Heads turned to identify the noise.

"What a woman!" Jon said to himself. "Here is someone who knows how to live. I should endeavor to be more like her."

He looked around and recognized the same place he had performed *Hamlet* the day before. Jon walked to a metal bench nearby and sat down. He knew it was time for Anne to shine.

Emma came out of the store a few minutes later wearing a nice pair of light blue shoes with a similar floral pattern that perfectly complimented her dress.

"I probably paid too much for these but sometimes the stars align and fate makes decisions for you," she said as she showed off her new shoes.

"Winsome style," Anne said. "I love them."

"Thanks! I convinced myself I would get extra karma

credit if I found a good use for my other shoes." She sat on the bench next to Anne and handed her a shopping bag containing the shoes she wore earlier. "These are for you."

"Are you sure?" Anne asked as she looked in the bag.

"You need them more than I do," Emma said. "I really want you to have them."

"Bless your heart, Emma," Anne said as she removed the shoes from the bag. "You are very generous. Thank you, thank you, thank you."

Anne slipped off the grey rubber clogs and put them in the bag, then slid into the blood-red shoes and buckled the ankle straps. Anne carefully stood up and tried not to fall over. The shoes lifted her heels about two inches above her toes.

"How do they look?" Anne asked with shoulders back and chin elevated.

"They look like they were made for your dress," Emma said. She put her sweater into the paper bag that previously held her shoes. "I'm so happy my shoes found a match because they don't really go with anything I have, besides this sweater. How do they feel?"

"Not as comfortable as the other ones, but I feel tall and powerful in these," Anne said.

"Comfort and power seldom go together," she said.

Anne practiced walking in the new heels and enjoyed the satisfying clacking noise the soles made against the sidewalk. Men turned their heads to look at the noise and were so drawn to the sight of two beautiful women, they forgot what they were doing and became clumsy.

After a minute of walking in the shoes, Anne's feet,

legs, and posterior throbbed with discomfort.

"Men will never know all the things we do to please them," Anne said. "The effort, labor, and painful contortions required to make myself pleasing to a man's eyes are wasted if my beauty becomes a barrier to fairness."

"Well said! If you're in pain, you hide it well," Emma said. "Tell me about your dress. It's absolutely gorgeous."

"Thank you," Anne said, running a hand over the smooth velvet surface. "I feel like I've had this dress forever. It's much older than it looks. I was a little afraid to wear it this morning because of all the attention it calls, but I wanted to feel young again. On the other hand, nothing shows your age like old clothes."

"Oh, come on, you're not that old," Emma said. "You look my age."

"I was born in eighty-three," Anne said.

"So was I," Emma said. "You look fantastic! Age is just a number, anyway. You're as old as you feel. I feel like I'm twenty-five years old. You'd never guess I'm creeping up on forty."

"I feel forty," Anne said.

"So do I sometimes," Emma admitted. "Most of the men I date run for the exit the minute they learn I'm over thirty and divorced. I should probably start dating men who are closer to my own age."

"You're divorced?"

"Well, I wouldn't be dating if I was still married," Emma said. "Speaking of big mistakes, do you ever wish you could jump inside a time machine and travel back to when you were younger? I think ten years would be just about right for me."

"Is that possible?" Anne asked. "I have to go back to the Renaissance."

"Go back?"

"I've always wanted to visit the Renaissance," Anne clarified. "Can a time machine take me there?"

"I know just the place," Emma said with a wide smile. "You can travel back to the Renaissance every evening at Shakespeare's Globe, just down the road from here."

"They rebuilt the Globe?" Anne asked. "I thought it was destroyed by fire."

"The original one was destroyed by a fire," Emma clarified. "The modern Globe is a replica that was built in 1997. If you haven't seen it, you should."

"I think I would enjoy that," Anne said. "Do they still perform plays by William Shakespeare?"

"Tonight's play is *Twelfth Night*," Emma said.

Anne tried to remember some lines and spoke the first words that came to mind.

"I do I know not what, and fear to find mine eye too great a flatterer for my mind," Anne recited. "Fate, show thy force: ourselves we do not owe; what is decreed must be, and be this so."

"That's pretty good," Emma said. "I play Viola and Cesario."

"That's a real gender-bending role," Anne said.

"Sometimes I think it would be easier to be a man," Emma said. "I bet if I dressed and acted like a man I could do anything I wanted and no one would be the wiser."

"People expect a man to be stronger, braver, and more responsible than a woman," Anne said. "That's why women are called the weaker sex. Both men and women are much more likely to help a woman in need than a man. A helpless man is pathetic."

"People see what they want to see, and a woman can be every bit as strong and brave as a man," Emma said. "We let men think they're the stronger sex, but they can be such babies at times. Imagine a man menstruating every month. Ha!"

"I know exactly what you mean," Anne said. "I am perfectly capable of opening doors for myself, but I still think it's nice when a man holds a door open for me. It gives him an opportunity to be chivalrous, which is a good thing. I like to let men do nice things for me."

"Unless he's doing it to make himself feel superior," Emma said. "I don't need to reinforce some loser's hero fantasy."

"That fantasy might be all he has left," Anne said. "Men may transform into beasts or to heroes if given the opportunity. It's the same for women, but the expectations are different. If men had the curse once a moon, women would be the ones holding doors open."

"I hope you realize that life was much harder for women in the past," Emma said. "Women had no rights, we couldn't vote, we didn't go to university, we couldn't act onstage, and we couldn't own property unless it was inherited or we married a man with property. Trust me, modern life is much better for women than it was in the Renaissance."

"Women can do all of those things today?" Anne asked. "That's wonderful! But then why would you want to dress up as a man if a woman has the same rights? Men are swine."

"Because they are swine," Emma said. "No one gave women equal rights; we demanded them. Women are just as strong as men or stronger, and I can prove it. We don't need a man's money or his patriarchy."

"You seem so confident," Anne said. "I hate to ask for another favor after all you've done for me."

"What is it?"

"Can you lend me some money?" Anne asked. "I woke up this morning in such a hurry I grabbed the wrong shoes and forgot my purse. I'd rather ask you than a man."

Emma looked through her purse and handed Anne two fifty-pound notes.

"This is too much," Anne said, handing back one bill.

"We girls need to help each other," Emma said as she rejected the bill. "You can pay me back later."

"Are you sure? This is such a relief. Thank you!"

"You should come see me perform tonight at the Globe," Emma said. "I think you would really enjoy it. Unfortunately, I have to get to work, and I'm already super late. It was great meeting you, Anne."

The two new friends hugged goodbye. Their hug felt wonderful and Anne wanted another.

"Likewise, Emma," Anne said. "Thank you for everything. You are an inspiration, and I shan't forget it. I promise I will try to come see you tonight."

Anne watched Emma walk away and planned the next

move. The shoes gave Anne a new sense of authority and confidence that came at the cost of intense physical discomfort that no one else knew or cared about. Anne decided women must have a much higher pain threshold than men if they can have babies and walk on high heels. Anne stood, recognized and accepted the pain for what it was, and moved forward despite it.

Anne found a nearby clothing store dedicated entirely to men's new and used suits named "The Bespoke Bunker." The inside of the store was filled with men's suits of all colors and materials. The suits were arranged on long racks by common color and pattern, and organized by size with like colors.

"May I help you find something, ma'am?" asked a porter. Anne was the only customer in the store.

"Yes, I hope so," Anne said. "I wish to be fitted for a gentleman's suit, and I'm on a limited budget."

"We have a wide range of excellent items and hopefully we can find something you like," he said. "May I ask how limited?"

"Less than one hundred pounds," Anne said.

"We have a number of very nice, gently used suits at that price point," the tailor said. He helped Anne loosen and remove the dress, petticoat, and corset. Next, he measured Anne's shoulders, chest, waist, and inseam.

After trying on several different suits that were the right size, Anne found a three-piece suit in navy blue that required no adjustments. It was made of Scottish tweed wool, stitched in a herringbone pattern.

The tailor said the suit was about fifty years old, but

it was still in fine condition. He found a white dress shirt, a black necktie, and a pair of used leather shoes that fit well, but needed a good polish. The tailor had to teach Anne how to tie the necktie in a full Windsor knot. He placed a folded white handkerchief into the jacket's breast pocket, and Jon's transformation was complete.

"Now you look like a proper English gentleman," the tailor said. "I guarantee you will still be turning heads. A suit like this will open doorways to new possibilities. I hope you are ready for a big change. Good luck!"

Chapter Seven

For the first time in more than 400 years, Jon emerged onto the street dressed as a gentleman. He was anxious to see the Globe rebuilt, but he was hungry and had a few hours to kill before the performance began.

Jon read the menu and prices hanging in the window of a nice restaurant to see if he could afford anything. He checked his remaining financials and verified he had enough cash for dinner somewhere else cheaper.

He returned to his favorite fast-food restaurant and ordered another fish sandwich. Jon got his hair cut at a barbershop and had his leather shoes polished. He took a walk along the riverbank and watched the boats and ships pass between the tall buildings.

Jon stopped at the shelter by the church and put the dress, corset, and petticoat into a storage locker. He used his last one-pound coin to access a secure locker and put the key in his pocket.

He ventured toward the place where he expected to find the Globe Theatre but the streets and buildings were different, and he was disoriented. When Jon finally saw the theater, it was not what or where he expected.

The three-story, cylindrical building was made of

timber and white-washed mud that sharply contrasted the surrounding architecture of glass and steel facades. Jon thought it looked like it could be a Renaissance theater or a bull-baiting establishment. Huge billboards outside the theater displayed Shakespeare's portrait and his signature.

Jon approached the box office and stood in the queue to get a ticket for the Friday evening performance of *Twelfth Night.* A sign said gallery seating started at forty pounds, whereas a spot standing in the yard as a groundling cost just five pounds.

Jon wasn't sure how much money he had left, and he emptied his pockets onto the ticket counter. He was out of paper bills and one-pound coins, but he still had a pile of smaller change. Jon counted out 480 pence worth of coins, but that was all he had. He was broke.

"It looks like I'm still short about seven hundred pence," Jon told the box office porter. "I remember back when it cost one pence to see a play in the yard and sixpence for a seat in the galleries."

"You are short twenty pence," the porter said after counting all the coins.

Jon wasn't clear if the porter was a man or a woman, but they had short black hair like a man, wore makeup including black lip gloss and eyeliner, and had multiple facial piercings. The porter was in their early twenties and wore a denim vest over a white shirt and black leather pants. Their name tag said "Reece."

"I thought you said it was five pounds," Jon said. "This is only about two pounds. Does not twelve pennies make a shilling and twenty shillings make a pound?"

"That was before decimalization," Reece said, tiredly. "I don't know what a shilling is. There are a hundred pennies to a pound. You are only twenty pennies short of five pounds."

"I will pay the difference," said the person standing in the queue behind Jon. "I'm terrible with counting change, too. It's much easier to pay with plastic."

"You don't have to do that, but I appreciate it," Jon said to the person behind him. "Thank you."

"It's only twenty pence," the person said. "Don't worry about it. Enjoy the show."

Jon thanked the person, took his ticket, and went to find a good place to stand in the yard. There was plenty of room inside. He felt an odd sensation upon entering the theater – simultaneously new and familiar.

His last memories were of the theater in ashes, yet here it was, rebuilt as if nothing had happened. It felt much more sterile and sanitized than Jon remembered, and there were new things like safety rails and lighted exit signs. The roof was thatched. Jon wasn't sure if he was in the right place at the wrong time or the wrong place at the right time. There was something artificial about the building, yet it also felt like it could be home, with a few adjustments and a little imagination.

Jon stood on the concrete floor next to the stage and watched as the wealthier patrons filled the gallery seats and the other groundlings like himself filled the yard. The theater was nearly filled to capacity with about 1,500 patrons when the play began. A band of musicians came on stage playing a song with lutes and flutes for a well-dressed duke. When the song finished, the duke began:

"If music be the food of love, play on; give me excess of it, that, surfeiting, the appetite may sicken, and so die."

The tall bearded actor playing the duke continued pining over the unrequited love of his lady, and the first scene ended. Jon recognized Emma the minute she came on stage.

Viola was lost in a strange land after being shipwrecked and separated from her twin brother. Having few options as a woman, she vowed to serve the duke as a castrated male servant called a eunuch.

With the aid of a mustache and goatee, Viola assumed the identity of a handsome young man named Cesario and quickly gained favor with the duke.

As the two drunken knights in the third scene plotted to enlist their servants in creating mischief, Jon remembered Will once told him he mixed commoners with nobility in his plays to better reach the entire audience, and because fools and drunks could get away with saying things that his heroes could not.

The audience was laughing at most of the jokes and puns, but Jon thought the actors were waiting for the laughter to fade before they delivered their next lines. He was not accustomed to waiting for a reaction and thought it made the pace of the play considerably slower. Jon noticed the actors pronounced a lot of words differently and many of the rhymes didn't work anymore.

The play ended several hours later as the servant Malvolio vowed revenge on his tormentors. Jon lingered around the stage while the other spectators headed for the exits. After a few minutes, Jon was the last person in the theater. He was admiring the interior when the bearded actor who played the duke noticed Jon still in the audience.

"Are you alright?" he asked Jon. "The show's over."

"I'm admiring your theater," Jon said. "It looks remarkably similar to the original."

"The structure was designed to be as authentic as possible," he said. "The framing was made from oak beams with interlocking mortise and tenon joints."

"I noticed the roof is thatched," Jon said. "Aren't you worried about a fire?"

"There are water sprinklers installed in the ceilings that will activate during a fire," he said.

"Remarkable," Jon said. "Would it be possible to get a tour of the theater complex some time?"

"We offer guided tours on weekday mornings," he said. "Are you an architect or historian?"

"I'm a fellow actor," Jon said. "I greatly enjoyed your play tonight, and I might be in love with your theater."

"Some of us actors are going out for drinks at a pub around the corner called Ganymede's," he said. "You should stop by and introduce yourself. I need to get out of my costume, and the night crew needs to clean the theater. Maybe I'll see you later."

"See you later," Jon said. He left the theater and contemplated what to do next.

Jon seriously considered going back to the shelter for the night. It was almost dark and the beds filled up quickly. The shelter turned away anyone who smelled of alcohol or drugs, and Jon remembered he was drugged the last time he went to a pub. Despite the risks, he decided to check it out. His entire career had revolved around the Globe, and now he had an opportunity to live that lifestyle again.

Ganymede's was a clean and spacious restaurant. The lights were dimmed, and each table had a spotlight on its center. There was a bar that ran the length of the restaurant. Every table at the restaurant was presently filled with diners, and there was a waiting list to get the next table. There were still a few empty seats at the bar. Jon sat on one of the bar stools and picked up a menu. All the food was Greek and had Greek-sounding names.

The back wall was lined with different kinds of hard liquor Jon had never heard of, and the mixed drinks were even more exotic. He was so happy to be back in society he wished he could buy everyone a drink. Instead, he did his best to be temperate and ordered an ice water.

Emma came in to the bar with another woman Jon thought he recognized. Emma was wearing the same blue floral dress and shoes from earlier. She had washed off her stage makeup and had her regular makeup on. Jon thought he could have a future with Emma, and the idea of his future woke up new feelings inside him.

Her friend was wearing a T-shirt that said "Take me to your leader," topped with an unzipped black leather jacket. She wore tight blue jeans and black boots. Emma was about the same height as Jon and her friend was about a walnut taller. Jon thought she looked like a Spanish leather dealer. He recognized her as the actress who played Olivia in *Twelfth Night*.

Jon knew Emma also played Cesario but he couldn't

see the resemblance now that she was out of character. Jon made eye contact with Emma and smiled and waved at her. Emma and her friend came over.

"Have we met?" Emma asked Jon as she took the empty bar stool next to him. "You look familiar."

"I saw you both in *Twelfth Night* tonight. My name is Jon Henry."

"I'm Emma Morgan."

"Carmen Sandoval."

"Good to meet you," Jon said and shook their hands. "You two were terrific tonight."

"Thank you," Carmen said. "Are you a critic?"

"I'm a fellow actor," Jon said. "I have done *Twelfth Night*, and the gender switch can be a real bear on the loose."

"How do you mean?" Emma asked.

"Like a bear in the crowd," he said. "Unpredictable."

"How did we do against the bear?" Carmen asked.

"Against?" Jon asked.

"Cesario is the bear on the loose," Emma said.

"Metaphorically," Jon said. "Bears can be terrifying if you don't know what to expect and you have only heard bad things about bears. Viola wanted to be strong like a bear but to do that she had to pretend to be someone's fantasy instead of being herself."

"Whose fantasy did Cesario fulfill?" Emma asked.

"Definitely Olivia's fantasy," Carmen said and then she joked with Emma, "You're so dreamy, Cesario."

"Cesario was a woman's ideal man," Jon said. "Viola knew exactly what a woman wants to hear from a man, which is praise of herself and nothing else."

Jon reached for Emma's hand and she gave it to him. He felt his own heartbeat quicken as he held her hand and quoted one of Cesario's lines to her.

"'Lady, you are the cruelest she alive, if you will lead these graces to the grave and leave the world no copy,'" Jon said.

"That's because men only want to talk about themselves and their own feelings," Emma said, and she withdrew her hand from his. "Men would rather hear what other men think than hear what a woman thinks."

"Is that why Viola put on a disguise to meet the duke in the beginning?" Jon asked.

"Viola knew she would have to be tough to survive in Illyria, and she didn't want to be a burden to anyone," Emma said. "She decided to be Duke Orsino's servant when she couldn't serve Olivia. A bachelor duke can't have a female advisor, so she disguised herself."

"Twas very brave of her," Jon said, "but there are consequences to living outside of society's expectations."

"I feel like we've met before," Emma said. "Even though we just met, I can tell I like you, Jon, and I will allow you to buy me a drink if you feel so inclined."

"You may buy us both drinks, Jon," Carmen added and flashed him a coy smile.

Jon smiled nervously. Despite his dapper appearance, Jon had no money, no job or income, and no home or property. He really liked Emma but couldn't afford to buy her anything. He owed her £100 and still had her shoes. But it was more than that. Emma gave him a chance. He felt he owed her everything.

"I would give you the moon if it were mine to bestow," Jon said as he looked into Emma's eyes. "Not the moon that disappears in the morning, nor the moon that waxes to full brightness and then wanes to nothing a few weeks later. I want to be your moon for the ages."

"Ganymede is a moon of Jupiter," Emma said as she looked into Jon's eyes. "It's bigger than Earth's moon and larger than the planet Mercury. You can be Zeus, king of the gods, and I will be Ganymede, your cupbearer. Shall I fetch thou a drink?"

Jon was surprised by Emma's generosity and her knowledge of the heavens. Jon wondered if he could stop at just one drink. His doctor had advised him never to drink alcohol again. One drink might not kill him, but the last drink he had almost did. Jon wanted to accept her offer, but he felt like there was too much at risk.

"I appreciate the offer," Jon said. "But we only just met. We don't know anything about each other."

"That's what the drink is for," Carmen said. "It breaks the ice and keeps things flowing."

"Can I get you both an ice water?" he asked. "That's what I'm having. Let's break our ice together."

Jon ordered another two glasses of complimentary ice water with a lemon wedge. When Emma and Carmen had their waters, Jon raised his to make a toast.

"Here's to secret identities," he said.

"To secret identities," both women repeated.

Jon began to take a sip of water and then he added, "May they never be divulged."

Emma and Carmen both giggled as they took a drink.

The actor who played Duke Orsino came in to the bar wearing a black leather jacket and blue jeans. He recognized Emma and Carmen and came over to join the three of them.

"Everything good?" the man asked.

"Good so far," Carmen said. "I learned that Ganymede is larger than Mercury."

"Hi, I'm Steve," he said to Jon and extended his hand.

Jon stood up to shake his hand. Steve was much taller, with broad shoulders and a manly beard that covered his square jaw. Steve had brown eyes and short brown hair with blond highlights, and a handsome face. Jon thought Steve looked like an English leather merchant.

"Hi Steve, I'm Jon," Jon said as he shook Steve's hand with a firm grip. "We met earlier. I thought your Orsino was well delivered, and I felt a little envious that you got to marry the heroine at the end."

"Thanks," Steve said. He looked at Carmen. "Hey, babe," he said, then kissed her on the lips. Steve sat in the empty seat next to Carmen. Jon was surprised they were a couple until he noticed their outfits matched.

"We were talking about the play, and Jon said he is a fellow actor," Emma said.

"You mentioned that to me earlier," Steve said. "Where do you work?"

"It's embarrassing to say, but I'm presently out of work," Jon said. "Hopefully that will change soon. I once worked at the Globe, many years ago."

"We've all been out of work before," Steve said.

"You just have to keep trying. Maybe we can put in a good word for you; let you get your foot in the door. It's a shot."

"I would really like to act at the Globe again," Jon said. "I can do any role. It doesn't matter."

"The Globe is having auditions for our next play on Monday morning," Emma said. "You should try out."

"We can get you in, but the director will decide if you have what it takes to be a Globe actor," Carmen said.

"I will be there Monday morning," Jon said. "Thank you for this opportunity, and I hope we can all make magic onstage someday."

Carmen gave her smartphone to Steve and had him stretch his arm out to take a group photo of all four of them at the bar. Steve handed the device back to Carmen, and she began tapping on it excitedly. She whispered something to Emma and then to Steve, and they both nodded in agreement.

"This is short notice, but are you free tomorrow?" Steve asked. "We're going to a Renaissance festival in Stratford. Would you like to join us or meet us there?"

"Stratford-upon-Avon?" Jon said. "I haven't been there in ages. I don't see how I could possibly meet you there by tomorrow. That's a three-day ride by horse."

"We're taking my car," Emma said. "Meet us at the Globe tomorrow morning at eight if you want a ride."

"We might be colleagues in the near future," Jon said. "We could become competitors. Is it wise to fraternize?"

"Don't worry about it," Steve said. "Maybe you'll make a friend. What are you guys drinking?"

"Ice water," Carmen said.

"To break the ice," Emma said. "It's working."

"Bartender, this is the best water I have ever tasted," Jon proclaimed, and everyone laughed.

They chatted until the bar area got too loud and crowded. Steve took Carmen home on his motorcycle, and Jon walked Emma to her neighborhood.

"Carmen and Steve are what happens when the most popular girl at theater school dates the most popular boy," Emma said. "They look great together but I wonder what else is going on. They're both doing Shakespeare to pad their resumes for their future film careers, not because they love Shakespeare."

"Maybe their relationship is also driven by a mutual desire that does not require a love of the subject," Jon said.

"I need more than a mutual desire," Emma said as she came to a stop at a well-lit street corner. "This is my neighborhood. Thanks for walking me home, Jon."

"It was my pleasure," Jon said as he shook her hand. "Until tomorrow."

Jon turned in the direction of the shelter and started to walk when Emma called after him. He turned to face her.

"The festival will have costumes you can rent if you don't have your own," she said. "The Globe also has a bunch of Renaissance outfits that cast members can borrow. Come early and I'll let you pick one out."

"I will," he called back. "Thank you!"

Jon retraced his steps back to Ganymede's and then to the shelter next to Southwark Cathedral. The facility was at capacity, but they let Jon sleep inside on the floor. He removed his tweed jacket, tie, and vest and used them as a pillow. He was asleep before they turned the lights out, and woke up at dawn.

He was lucky enough to get a cup of coffee that the shelter volunteers offered for free to the early risers, but there were no muffins or pastries left. Jon couldn't wait to get back to the Globe.

Emma was unlocking the back door to the theater when Jon arrived. She was wearing blue denim jeans and a grey sweatshirt that said RADA on the front.

"Good morning, Emma," Jon said. "Can I lend you a hand?"

"Jon!" Emma said. She walked over to Jon and gave him a hug. "I'm glad you came. I don't like being here by myself. Carmen and Steve will probably get here at the last minute. Let me show you the Renaissance costumes we can borrow for the day."

Emma led Jon through a different building connected to the back of the theater and into a room labeled "wardrobe." She turned on the lights and the room was filled with hundreds of period costumes. There were doublets, jerkins, and girdles for the men and corsets, petticoats, and dresses for the women.

"Some of these are quite nice," Jon said. "Why are we getting dressed up?"

"To pretend we're living in the Renaissance," she said. "It's about three hundred people gathering for a day of food, music, games, and contests. They have a contest for most authentic Renaissance man and woman, and contestants are judged on a wide range of categories. Carmen told me she wants to win the women's contest and she probably will. She usually gets what she wants."

Jon found a blue doublet and breeches that were very similar to his old clothes he lost in the fire. He took off his blue tweed suit and put it in a locker. Next, Jon put on a girdle, pulled up his white stockings to his knees, then got into the breeches and doublet. He found a blue cap and cape, as well as a rapier sword he wore about his waist. He examined his appearance in a full-length mirror and thought he looked like his old self again.

"Blue is a good color on you," Emma said. "The hat and cape are a nice touch. Is that a real sword?"

"I think it's hollow," Jon said. "It feels too light."

Emma looked at the rapier.

"It's plastic," she said. "If it looks real, it's close enough. Don't use it for actual sword fighting."

"Is that what you're wearing?" Jon asked.

Emma was still wearing her sweatshirt and jeans.

"No. I can't wear my outfit while I'm driving, so I'll bring it and get changed when we get there," Emma said.

Steve pulled up to the back of the Globe on his motorcycle with Carmen seated behind him. Carmen got off the motorcycle and took off her helmet while Steve parked in the theater's secure lot. They were both wearing the same leather jackets and denim jeans as the night before. Steve removed his helmet.

"Good to see thou again, Steve," Jon said as he shook Steve's hand.

"You too," Steve said. "I like your doublet. The cape might be a little overkill."

"You think so?" Jon asked. "I considered wearing a

jerkin but I didn't see one I liked. It's much warmer without the polar ice caps. I don't even need one."

"I need to find a costume," Steve said and went inside.

"You look handsome, Jon," Carmen said as she came over to Jon and gave him a hug. "Have you been to the Stratford Renaissance Festival before?"

"I was born in Stratford-upon-Avon," Jon said. "I never knew there was a festival until last night. I have no idea what to expect."

"Emma can tell you," Carmen said. "I need to change into my favorite Renaissance dress. See you soon!"

"Anon," Jon said and waved at Carmen as she went inside the theater. He looked at Emma.

"I told you: it's an all-day costume party with a Renaissance theme," she said. "You can be a Renaissance man for a day or just be yourself, as long as you have fun. My costume is in the car already. You can sit up front with me or sit in the back with Steve. I don't think Steve would like it if you sat with Carmen."

"I'd love to sit up front with you," Jon said. "I've seen these around but I've never been inside one before."

"A Camry?" Emma asked. "It's comfortable and it runs well." She opened the passenger door for him.

"Is it safe?" he asked as he sat in the passenger seat on the left side. Emma sat in the driver's seat.

"Camrys are some of the safest cars out there," she said. "Did you notice any dents on the outside of the car?"

"No, I did not."

"I've owned this car for about eight years and it doesn't have dents or scratches because I'm a safe driver,"

Emma said. “Also, I hardly drive anywhere.”

“This is very nice,” Jon said as he felt the leather interior and made himself comfortable. He watched Carmen exit the backstage dressed in a slender white satin dress with gold brocade accents. She wore leather sandals and a beautiful pearl necklace. Jon could tell from the way Carmen moved that she was wearing a bodice underneath. She got in the back seat on the left side behind Jon.

“Killer dress, Carmen,” Emma said as she looked into the rearview mirror and made eye contact with Carmen’s reflection.

“Thanks,” Carmen said. “I went with a Mediterranean look because it compliments my skin tone. I hope it doesn’t look too southern.”

“The Renaissance was in Europe, too,” Emma said.

“What if someone confuses you for being a Catholic?” Jon asked.

“I am Catholic,” Carmen said.

Jon was stunned. She was the first Catholic he knew.

Steve exited the theater dressed in a yellow doublet with yellow-and-white-striped breeches and long white stockings covering his legs. He wore a large sleeveless faux-fur coat over the doublet. Steve made sure the theater was locked and the car park was secure, then he got in the back seat on the right side, next to Carmen.

“Everybody ready?” Emma asked. “Seatbelts on. Next stop: Stratford-upon-Avon.”

Jon needed a moment to find his seatbelt and figure out how to buckle it, and had to look at Emma’s seat belt to see how it should go.

Once everyone was ready, Emma turned on the car and pulled out into the street. Jon's eyes were huge as he looked out the different windows, and he kept turning in his seat as he watched objects fly past them until they were out of view. He began to feel nauseous as he tried to watch everything from the moving vehicle.

Jon recognized a few places they passed when they started moving, but after a few minutes, he was completely disoriented. Every place in the city started to look the same. Emma was focused on driving, and Carmen and Steve were both looking down at their smartphone devices in the back seat. Jon tried looking straight ahead.

"My driving isn't that bad, is it?" Emma asked as they waited for a red light to turn green. "You look nervous."

"My apologies," Jon said. "You seem to be proficient at operating a Camry, but I'm not used to it yet. How long will this take?"

"Once we get outside the city, it should take about ninety minutes to get there," she said.

Soon the buildings disappeared and the countryside became flat and green.

The vehicles moving on the right side of the road in the opposite direction seemed to be traveling incredibly fast. Jon grew weary and stared straight ahead.

Emma turned a dial and some music began to play from the car. The music made him sleepy.

"Would you mind if I rested my eyes?" Jon asked after a while. "I trust your driving."

"That's fine," she said.

Jon closed his eyes. After a few minutes, his head

began to bob. He leaned against the door and fell asleep. After a few minutes of driving in silence, Emma spoke.

"You're pretty cute, Jon, but you also seem pretty clueless," Emma said. She looked in the rearview mirror to confirm Steve and Carmen were also napping in the back seat.

"Is this an act, or are you really a gentleman?" Emma continued. "You seem to know your Shakespeare, but you've never heard of a Renaissance festival, you've never been inside a Camry before, and you think it's a three-day horse ride to Stratford? You're not the only man who looks sexy in a doublet. I think you are about to get an education."

Chapter Eight

Jon awoke from a nap to see he was still in Emma's car traveling to Stratford-upon-Avon, but they were no longer on the busy highway and were traveling on a two-lane country road past forests, farms, and cottages.

"We're almost there," Emma said. "Did you sleep?"

"I don't remember," Jon said. "It feels like I just closed my eyes for a minute. How long was I asleep?"

"Most of trip," Emma said. "Carmen and Steve had a nap too. Are you guys ready?"

"Yeah, let's do this," Steve said.

"When and where are we meeting to go home?" Carmen asked.

"Good questions," Emma said. "We will meet back at the car at five o'clock to return to London. Don't be late."

"How will I know what time it is?" Jon asked.

"You really don't have a watch or a cell phone?" Carmen asked.

"No."

"They didn't have smartphones in the Renaissance," Steve joked. "You'll be fine without one."

"I suggest you ask someone for the time so you don't miss your ride," Emma said.

She made a few turns and found an empty parking space near the bandstand and next to a huge grassy recreation field on the eastern bank of the Avon. Jon could see large tents set up for the festival.

"I have to put on my costume before I go in, so I'll see you all in there," Emma said when they exited the car. "Remember to meet here at five o'clock. Have fun!"

Jon, Steve, and Carmen walked to the gate together. Jon paused to read the admission pricing. It cost twenty pounds for adults, and fifteen pounds for children and seniors. There were costumes available to rent.

"Do you have enough to get in?" Carmen asked. Jon shook his head. "I'll spot you this time and you can pay me back later."

"Are you sure?" Jon asked. Carmen smiled and nodded. "Thank you! It's embarrassing being broke."

Carmen paid for herself and Jon, and Steve bought his own ticket. They both paid with credit cards. The porter stamped the back of their hands with blue ink in the shape of the comedy and tragedy faces, the muses Thalia and Melpomene.

Steve took Jon aside for a moment.

"The entertainment is included but everything else here costs money," Steve said as he discretely handed Jon a folded twenty-pound note. "We brought you up here for Emma, so maybe you can buy her something when you see her. We'll see you inside."

"Much obliged, Steve," Jon said.

Jon looked at a trifold brochure with a map of the festival and starting times for the various performances.

He could only guess the approximate time from the morning sun and decided to visit the vendor tents first.

Beneath an enormous red-and-white-striped tent were more than four dozen vendor booths that featured arts and crafts made by independent area artisans.

Jon explored the various pottery, wood, and metal art for sale, as well as replica weapons, leather and chainmail metal armor, and costume dresses made of silk and velvet materials. There were fantasy paintings of dragons for sale, as well as handmade jewelry and a wide assortment of bath and beauty products. Very few items cost less than twenty pounds and most of the nicer items sold for hundreds of pounds.

He kept exploring and came to the vendors who specialized in wearable fairy wings, elf ears, horns, or antlers. There was a wide assortment of supplies for wizards and witches of all ages, including wands, brooms, and books of magic spells.

Jon feared he might be surrounded by real witches and wizards and began to feel paranoid and superstitious. Then he saw people dressed as steampunk pirates and space aliens. Everyone else was dressed in modern clothing. Jon began to feel confused about what was real and what was a fantasy. He knew he needed to escape to a quiet place.

He left the large tent and walked across the lawn to the riverbank. There were ducks and geese floating in the water, and Jon stood for a few minutes watching the birds and the flowing current. It was cool in the shade next to the Avon, and the breeze felt nice. The babbling current drowned out both the noise from the festival behind him and the city noises from the other side of the river.

Jon relaxed and let his mind go blank. He didn't notice the man approach the riverbank from his back.

"You look like you're suffering from anachronistic shock," said a man's voice from behind Jon. "I hate that. I bet I can bring you back to your proper time period."

Jon turned around and saw a gentleman dressed like himself in a doublet and breeches, with a cap, cape, and rapier. Instead of wearing all blue, this gentleman was dressed in alternating colors of crimson and blue. He had short brown hair and a reddish-brown mustache and goatee. The man tipped his cap to Jon and smiled.

"There weren't pirates, space aliens, or wizards and witches the last time I was in the Renaissance," Jon said with a smile. "I understand that times have changed, but it's confusing to an old-timer like me."

"I know what you mean," the man said. "I've been going to these festivals since I was a child and I don't remember there being any wizards or aliens back then. I guess the Renaissance period isn't fun enough for everyone."

"Oh, it definitely wasn't fun for everyone," Jon said. He extended his hand. "I'm Jon Henry."

"Ryan Morgan," he replied, reaching out to shake Jon's hand. "Good to meet you."

Jon observed he and Ryan were approximately the same size and height, the same age, and they appeared to have equal social status. Ryan had the comedy/tragedy stamp from the festival on the back of his hand.

"I don't remember the Avon being this clean before,"

Shakespeare On Ice

JM

Jon said as he continued to watch the waterfowl. "I used to fish along these banks as a boy. The world was a simpler time back then."

"Did you grow up here?" Ryan asked.

"We had a house in town when I was a boy, but it burned to the ground in a fire," Jon said. "My parents sent me to London to study. I never really considered Stratford-upon-Avon my home again."

"I grew up in Oxford, and like you, I moved to London to study," Ryan said. "I'm happier in London, much to the disappointment of my parents, who continually insist I move back to Oxford and settle down. I'm too young to settle down."

"I felt the same way myself not too long ago," Jon said. "I was in my prime and saw retirement as some far-away idea to worry about later. I thought that my life would wait for when I was ready. But I was wrong. I should have listened to Will and got out when I still had the chance. Now he's gone, and I'm too late."

"I'm sorry for your loss," Ryan said.

"I thought I would have more time," Jon said. "Now it seems I do. I'm back at the city of my birth and the city where my friend is buried. There are ghosts everywhere I look. I need to make peace with my past before I can think about my future."

"Your friend Will is buried in here in Stratford-upon-Avon?" Ryan asked.

"That's what I heard," Jon said.

"Do you know where he's buried?" Ryan asked. "We can visit his grave together."

"Not exactly," Jon said. "I do appreciate your help."

"What's your friend's last name? We can start there."

"Shakespeare," Jon said.

"Your friend is William Shakespeare, the poet and playwright?" Ryan asked. "The Bard of Avon?"

"Yes, that's him," Jon said.

Ryan frowned, and watched the river for a moment.

"OK, I'll play along," Ryan said. "Shakespeare is buried in Holy Trinity Church." He pointed south down the river at a medieval church with a pointy spire on the opposite bank.

"Would you care to take a walk with me?" Jon asked.

"Sure," Ryan said. "It's a fine day for a walk to Shakespeare's church."

They began walking together along the riverbank toward the church. Their pace was slow, like the current.

"Are you here alone or with friends?" Ryan asked.

"I came here with some friends from London, but I don't see any of them at present," Jon said. "How about yourself?"

"I drove from London this morning as well, just for this festival," Ryan said. "What do you do in London?"

"I'm an actor," Jon said. "Currently out of work but working to change that. And you?"

"I'm in advertising," Ryan said. "I probably could have guessed you're an actor."

"Is it obvious?" Jon asked.

"Renaissance festivals were made for creative people like us," Ryan said. "I would be more worried if you weren't an actor. Where did you study acting?"

"It had many names," Jon said. "'Children of the Chapel' was one name. We were all boys, but we played parts for men and women of all ages."

"You've been acting since childhood?" Ryan asked.

"I was chosen," Jon said. "All of us boys were chosen but only a handful of us had what it took to become a professional actor. The younger actors looked up to me, and I looked up to the older boys. Many of us remained friends when we were adults."

They reached a wooden footbridge that crossed the river and Holy Trinity Church was on the opposite side. Jon went across first and Ryan followed.

"What did he tell you?" Ryan asked when he reached the other side. Jon was confused, so Ryan clarified: "What did Shakespeare tell you that you should have listened to but didn't? Forgive my curiosity."

They arrived at the church's main entrance.

"Will said he was quitting the theater life and coming here to grow old and fat," Jon said. "He told me I should join him."

Jon removed his cap and stepped inside. Ryan removed his cap and followed inside.

They crossed through the church's threshold into its vaulted interior. Large windows of stained glass were surrounded by elaborate stone tracery. They approached the chancel to the high altar where a vase filled with damask roses rested on the stone floor. A blue rope lay on the ground to outline a space surrounding the flowers, and a small sign marked Shakespeare's grave.

Jon was suddenly overwhelmed with grief and

collapsed to his knees on the floor in front of the marker. He could barely breathe as his reality crumbled to pieces.

The words carved in the stone epitaph were difficult to read as they were written upside-down, from the high altar's point of view. The words were repeated on a nearby sign, clearly written in large white letters against a black background.

"Good friend, for Jesus sake forebear, to dig the dust enclosed here," Ryan said as he read the inscription. "Blessed be the man who spares these stones, and cursed be he that moves my bones."

Jon rested on his knees and wept, then said a prayer for his late friend.

"He died in 1616," Jon said after reading the marker. "That was only three years after the Globe fire. Fifty-two is old, but it's not that old."

"Why do you think Shakespeare chose to have this curse as his epitaph instead of a line from one of his poems or plays?" Ryan asked.

"So that no one would disturb his grave," Jon said. He was still on his knees. "Looks like it worked, too."

Jon looked up to the large window above the altar and contemplated the portrayal of the crucified Jesus Christ surrounded by saints. Jon adored and worshiped the prophet who preached kindness and morality and stood up to authority. He also appreciated the symbolism of a soul being reborn for a higher calling. This was a second chance to live the life he had lost. Jon rose to his feet with renewed purpose.

Shakespeare's grave held a place of honor in the

chancel, and he was surrounded by the graves of his wife, a daughter, granddaughter, and their husbands. Jon and Ryan approved of the stone statue of Shakespeare holding a writing quill on the wall closest to Shakespeare's grave. They explored the rest of the church and praised the poetry and colorful windows, then went back outside.

"I think Shakespeare is in good hands," Ryan said. "What do you want to do next? Do you remember where your family home was before it burned down?"

"Ahead a few blocks," Jon said and pointed.

Jon and Ryan followed the old town road into the historic downtown and were soon surrounded by tall, timber-framed buildings with whitewashed plaster walls. The timbers were hundreds of years old and were painted black to protect them from the ravages of time and insects.

They arrived at the gate of a public garden area. The plants were flowering and the air smelled heavenly to Jon. He listened to a chickadee sing on the branch of a mulberry tree.

"This is where my house was," Jon said. "I almost feel like I'm back in 1603, except everything is so clean."

"It's the paved streets," Ryan said. "It really keeps the dirt down. Sanitation for water and sewer helps, along with removing farm animals from the city setting."

"That makes sense," Jon said. "They seem like good improvements, but I thought things would have changed a bit more. There's a skyscraper where my home was near London Bridge. A skyscraper! But not here. Look at this town. Nothing ever changes."

Jon and Ryan were browsing the retail shops and

bookstores downtown when a large white automobile pulled up next to them and stopped. A window slid down and a person inside called out to them, "Where is Anne Hathaway's Cottage?"

"I'm not from around here," Ryan said. "Sorry."

Jon tried to remember but was drawing a blank.

"The name doesn't sound familiar," he said. "Anne Hathaway? No, sorry."

"She's Shakespeare's wife," the person said.

"You mean Anne Shakespeare's cottage?" Jon asked. "I think the Shakespeares live at New Place over there."

Jon turned and pointed at the New Place Gardens down the street. Shakespeare's mansion was gone and had been replaced by a beautiful garden. Jon was puzzled. He looked at Ryan.

"Anne Hathaway was her maiden name," the person said. "It's a famous landmark."

"The Hathaway family has a nice cottage nearby in Shottery, about a mile west of here," Jon said.

"About a mile? Thank you," the person said. The window slid closed, and the automobile left a cloud of exhaust as it drove away.

"I think I have seen enough shops," Ryan said. "Shall we return to the festival? Grab a bite to eat?"

"Marvelous idea," Jon said.

They walked back to the church, crossed the same foot bridge, and made a straight line for the food tent. Ryan bought them each a smoked turkey leg that they gnawed on as they walked around the festival.

"How about a little target practice?" Jon asked when

they came to the archery range.

There were ten paper targets set against hay bales, placed fifty meters back from the archers in the center of the grassy field. Jon and Ryan watched as ten archers shot all their arrows, most of which had hit their targets. The archers stopped shooting and walked out to collect their arrows for the next group.

Next it was Jon and Ryan's turn. Jon was impressed by the craftsmanship of the long bows, the design of which had not been improved upon since medieval times. Modern compound bows were not allowed at the festival.

The archery advisor gave everyone a quick safety tutorial before they began. Jon was surprised the advisor was a young woman. She explained the terminology and how to properly use the equipment. She said archers came in all ages and skill levels.

The advisor had shoulder-length, blonde hair and was wearing a white chemise with the sleeves rolled up to her elbows. Over this, she wore a green, sleeveless dress that laced up the front. She wore multiple necklaces and bracelets and several leather belts that crisscrossed her chest and waist and held her quiver of arrows.

Jon thought she was cute and looked very stylish. Most of the other archers were dressed in modern clothing of short-sleeved shirts and short pants or skirts.

The targets had a small yellow circle in the center worth five points, a red ring worth four points, a larger blue ring worth three points, a wide black ring worth two points, and a white outer ring worth one point.

When it was time to start shooting, Jon picked up an

arrow and placed the nock in the bowstring, then sighted his paper target, took aim, pulled back the string, and let go, sending the arrow downrange and into the red ring of his target. Jon thought it wasn't perfect, but it was still a good shot.

"Bollocks!" Ryan shouted. Jon saw that Ryan had missed his target completely. The archery advisor was busy helping someone else.

"Watch my form as I shoot, and then I'll watch yours," Jon said. He lined up another arrow, focused on the center of the paper target, pulled back the string, and let go. His second arrow also hit the red area.

"You make it look easy," Ryan said.

"Spread your feet apart a little more," Jon said. Ryan adjusted his footing. "Raise your right elbow higher. Focus on your target, not the arrow. Pull back, and let go."

Ryan fired a second arrow and hit the white, outer circle at the bottom of the target.

"I hit it!" Ryan said.

"Much better," Jon said. "Remember what I told you about focusing on your target. Your arrow begins falling the moment you release it. You must compensate the arc and aim higher, the further away your target is, or your shot will be too low."

Jon lined up another arrow, aimed, and fired. This time he hit a bullseye in the smaller yellow circle in the center. He smiled.

Ryan lined up an arrow and aimed at his target.

"Remember to aim a little higher," Jon said.

Ryan adjusted and released. His arrow hit just above

the center of the target in the blue ring.

"Nice shooting," Jon said as he drew a fourth arrow. "You need more practice. A target is just a symbol. I like to imagine I have tracked a magnificent, young stag through the forest, and I only have moments before it sees me and escapes. If my first shot doesn't take it down, I could have to track my prey for hours. I aim for its heart."

Jon aimed and fired. Another bullseye.

"If you are not a hunter, you can imagine you are Cupid," Jon continued as Ryan prepared to shoot again. "Aim for the hearts of unsuspecting youth and drive the lovers mad with every bullseye. There are a few eligible ladies at this festival that I would enjoy piercing with my arrow, if you get my meaning."

Ryan aimed and fired, but he completely missed the target again.

"Imagine it's your last arrow and your enemy approaches," Jon said as he drew his fifth and final arrow. "You don't get another shot, so you have to make this one count. Everything that's happened up to now is all for naught if you miss, but you can't think about the past right now. You must put aside all your accomplishments and your hopes for the future. Concentrate all of your energy and intention on the present moment and the current task at hand. Nothing else matters."

Jon was quiet and motionless as he focused on his target. He raised his bow, pulled the arrow back, and let go. Another bullseye. Jon grinned.

"Focus on one thing and block everything else out," Ryan repeated. He drew an arrow, concentrated on his target, pulled back, and let go. Bullseye.

"That's some fine shooting, sir," the archery advisor said to Ryan.

"Thanks. I was taught by the best," Ryan said and smiled at Jon.

After the archers shot all their arrows, they walked downrange to collect them. All five of Jon's arrows were stuck in the center area of the target. Three of Ryan's arrows were in the target and the other two were in the grassy field nearby.

The archery advisor asked Jon his name, and she took his picture standing next to his target.

"You have the highest score of the day with twenty-three points," she told Jon. "You have a good shot at winning the Renaissance Man contest if you do well in the other categories."

Jon and Ryan returned their arrows for the next archers and exited the archery course. They inquired about the contest rules and were informed that the Renaissance Man/Woman contest was judged on five areas, each worth twenty points, for a total of one hundred points.

In addition to archery, contestants were judged on their knowledge of Renaissance history, their knowledge of quotations from plays by William Shakespeare, the historical accuracy of their outfit, and finally they would be judged on their skill at dancing.

"I only earned nine points at archery, but you have a chance to win the whole contest," Ryan said. "I think it would be fun to try to win, especially if you have a shot."

"This is fun," Jon admitted. "Let's start with the

history. I am inexcusably ignorant of far too many things to count, but I know the sixteenth and seventeenth centuries pretty well."

They each took a pencil and a paper quiz to fill out privately. Fortunately for Jon, the Renaissance history quiz was multiple choice. Jon began reading question one:

"Which English monarch had the longest reign of the Renaissance? a) Henry VII, b) Henry VIII, c) Elizabeth I, or d) Elizabeth II."

Jon had to remind himself that King James I was no longer alive. He wasn't sure when the Renaissance ended, but he knew Queen Elizabeth II was still on the currency. He circled "c" for Elizabeth I. He read the next question:

"Who was never married to Henry VIII? a) Catherine Howard, b) Catherine of Aragon, c) Catherine Parr, or d) Catherine Middleton."

Jon knew all six wives of Henry VIII. He didn't recognize the family name Middleton as being royal and circled "d." He read the third question:

"What was traditionally kept inside a codpiece? a) fish hooks, b) pieces of cod, c) bollocks or d) all of these."

Codpieces were already out of fashion by the turn of the seventeenth century and they certainly weren't used for storing food or fish hooks. He wasn't certain what bollocks were but Ryan had cursed it when he missed his target. Jon liked new curse words so he circled "c" and moved on to the fourth question:

"Where is poet and playwright William Shakespeare buried? a) Westminster Abbey, b) Holy Trinity Church, c) Southwark Cathedral, or d) no one knows for sure."

Jon had visited Will's grave a few hours earlier and circled "b." He read the fifth and final question:

"Which of these common garments for Renaissance women was not required to be worn at all times in public? a) bodice, b) bonnet, c) farthingale, or d) kirtle."

Jon knew a kirtle was another name for a dress and a bodice and farthingale were undergarments. Women wore bonnets in public but Jon didn't think it was ever required. He circled "b" and then turned in his quiz just as Ryan finished his own.

"I majored in the performing arts, not history," Ryan said when he had finished.

"It was easier than I expected," Jon said.

Next was the quiz identifying quotations from plays written by Shakespeare. Instead of multiple choices, there was a line below each quote to write the name of its respective play. Jon asked the judge if he could have someone write his answers for him.

"My shaky handwriting is worsened by my terrible spelling," Jon said. "If I can scarcely read it, I doubt you would be able to. I seek the assistance of a scribe."

A ten-year-old child with ginger hair and little knowledge of the works of Shakespeare volunteered to write Jon's answers for him. Jon read the first quotation:

"I dare do all that may become a man; who dares do more is none."

Jon told his scribe to write "*Macbeth*." He read the next quotation:

"How sharper than a serpent's tooth it is to have a thankless child!"

"No one knows more about thankless children than *King Lear*," Jon said to the child. Jon read the next quotation:

"If you prick us, do we not bleed? If you tickle us, do we not laugh? If you poison us, do we not die? And if you wrong us, shall we not revenge?"

"That's Shylock from *The Merchant of Venice*," Jon said. He read the fourth quotation:

"I had rather hear my dog bark at a crow than a man swear he loves me."

Jon laughed. "Beatrice, from *Much Ado About Nothing*." He read the final quotation:

"Now is the winter of our discontent made glorious summer by this sun of York."

"That's the opening of *The Life and Death of King Richard III*," Jon said. The red-headed child finished writing and handed the quiz back for Jon to read over. A few words were misspelled but otherwise it was accurate.

"This should be Venice, not Venus," Jon said and returned it for the correction. "I thank you for your service, young man."

"I'm not a young man," the child said. "I'm a girl."

"I beg your pardon, young lass," Jon said with a tip of his cap. "I thank you all the same."

Jon turned in his form while Ryan struggled to complete his. Ryan rejoined Jon after he finished.

"That was a good quiz," Ryan said. "I really had to think about a few of the quotations."

A white-haired woman in a white, Elizabethan dress approached Jon and Ryan and invited them both to have their costumes judged as part of the competition. The men were happy to oblige.

Jon received a full twenty points for his costume's historical authenticity. Ryan received a score of nineteen points for his outfit and lost only one point for not wearing historically accurate undergarments.

They watched costumed actors demonstrate common Renaissance work, such as barrel making, blacksmithing, spinning wool into yarn, washing clothing by hand, and crafting wooden furniture with hand tools.

A white-bearded man in a yellow doublet posted the names and scores of the contest leaders. Jon was leading the men with eighty-three points, followed by Steve in second place with seventy-three points. Ryan had sixty-eight points and was in fifth place. Carmen was leading the women's contest with seventy-five points and her closest contender had just sixty points.

The judges announced the final category of dancing would be next. The man in the yellow doublet said per tradition, the first to dance would be the man and woman who had accrued the most points. If they danced well together, they would receive enough points to clench the title, but if their dance was a disaster, the competitors with the next highest score would get an opportunity to upset the leaders.

"I don't think I'm going to stay for the dance," Ryan said. "I had a great time with you at the festival today, Jon. Thanks for your help with archery. I don't make new friends easily, and I feel like we might be kindred spirits."

"You mentioned you live in London," Jon said.

"Perhaps you would like to arrange to meet socially."

"That would be nice," Ryan said. "What's your number?"

"I don't understand," Jon said.

"Your phone number, so I can call you."

"I don't have a phone."

"E-mail? Social media? Standard mail?"

"I don't have any of that stuff," Jon said.

"Are you like a Luddite?"

"What's a Luddite?" Jon asked.

"Someone who is against new technology."

"Not deliberately," Jon said. "I haven't had time."

"I envy you," Ryan said. "How do I reach you?"

"I have auditions on Monday, so let's plan to meet at Ganymede's after five o'clock," Jon said. "It's a pub in Southwark."

"I know where it is," Ryan said. "I will plan to meet you on Monday at Ganymede's after five."

"Speaking of time, do you have the time on you?" Jon asked. "I have to catch a ride at five o'clock."

"The whole festival is over by five o'clock, so you still have enough time and you won't miss anything," Ryan said. "Good luck with your dance. Your partner looks pretty."

"Let me introduce you," Jon said and walked through the crowd of spectators. When he reached Steve and Carmen, he turned around to find that Ryan was gone.

"If it does not offend thee, might I have the honor of dancing with the lovely Carmen for the sake of the contest?" Jon asked Steve.

"Have fun," Steve said. "But watch out; I'm a pretty good dancer myself."

Jon shook Steve's hand and then turned to Carmen.

"May I have this next dance, milady?" Jon asked Carmen elegantly as he offered his elbow.

"It would be my pleasure," Carmen said as she placed her hand on his arm. They walked arm-in-arm to the center of the dance floor and turned to face each other. The players in the band began a traditional song from the Renaissance with lutes and stringed instruments, flutes, leather drums, and a tambourine.

Jon recognized the Tudor song "Greensleeves" and led Carmen in the traditional dance. Jon sang the first few verses of the ballad to her in iambic pentameter as they danced, and she smiled at him as though it was the first time anyone had ever sung to her while dancing.

"I have been ready at your hand,
To grant what-ever thou wouldst crav',
Oh, I have waged both life and land,
Your love and goodwill for to have."

Jon's clear voice and perfect pitch were testimonial to his five years of singing in a boys' choir. He continued singing the chorus as they danced:

"Greensleeves was all my joy,
Greensleeves was my delight,
Greensleeves was my heart of gold,
And who but milady Greensleeves."

He sung two more verses of the ballad and Carmen and a few other people joined in the chorus, but Jon was the only one who knew all of the original words. To him, the musicians finished playing the song halfway through the story, before Jon could sing the other three verses.

Jon and Carmen bowed to each other when the music ended. All the actors and spectators applauded their perfect dance. Everyone started talking at once. Soon the music resumed and the costumed actors joined them for the second dance and invited everyone else to join as well.

Carmen and Jon were having fun and continued dancing together for the second song, until Carmen spotted Steve dancing with another attractive young woman, and her demeanor changed. Jon noticed Carmen was staring at this other woman, and strategically steered their dancing to put them alongside Steve and his partner.

Jon recognized the other woman as the blonde archery advisor. She no longer had her bow or quiver of arrows.

"Oh, there you are, dear," Carmen said to Steve. "Jon, you are a wonderful dancer but I want to finish this dance with Steve. Pardon me."

Carmen cut in between Steve and the blonde woman and began dancing with Steve. Jon made eye contact with the other woman and smiled.

"I'm Jon," he said.

"I remember you," she said as she returned his smile. "Three bullseyes. I'm Alice."

"Would you care to dance, Alice?"

"I would love to," she said.

Jon and Alice danced well together, but Alice continued watching Steve dance with Carmen from across the room, and Jon couldn't help but look for Emma. He did not sing. The second song ended, and all the dancers bowed to each other while everyone else applauded. Jon realized he had not paid attention to his dance partner.

Alice was a little shorter than Jon and she had thin brown eyebrows, blue eyes, and a warm smile. She was clean, she smelled nice, and her hands felt a little too soft and delicate for an archery expert. Jon was interested in knowing more about Alice but he didn't want to pester her with questions.

"I like your dress," he said. "You are a good dancer."

"Thanks," she said. Alice stopped staring at Steve and turned her attention to Jon. "You're a good dancer, too. And archer. You're pretty good at a lot of things, Jon. Are you just here for the festival?"

"Yes. I came with my friends from London," Jon said.

"You're from London? I want to move there after I graduate."

"I was born here, but I've been in London for most of my life," Jon said. The music started at a slower tempo and they began dancing to the third song. "I think it's wonderful that women attend university. Are you a student with the Royal Shakespeare Company here?"

"No, I'm still in high school," Alice said. "I work at these festivals on the weekends with my parents."

Jon realized Alice was much younger than he first thought, and she would be living with her parents if she was unmarried. Jon would need to introduce himself to Alice's father if things were to go any further. What could he tell her about himself? That he was unemployed and homeless? That he had been frozen for four hundred years? Jon knew he was definitely too old for her. He said nothing for the rest of the slow dance. Alice laid her head on his shoulder.

The third dance ended and the dancers all bowed to their partners. Jon thanked Alice and wished her well.

Once the dancing portion ended, the judges calculated the final scores and updated the leaderboard. Carmen had a final score of ninety-five, Steve had a score of ninety-three, and Jon dominated the competition with 103 points.

The festival's actors portraying the king and queen came forward to present the awards to the victors. Jon and Carmen stood at the front of the stage next to the king and queen, where everyone could see them.

"Women of the Renaissance don't get the recognition they deserve in our history," announced the actress who was portraying the queen. "This award recognizes the wide range of talents that were necessary to succeed as a Renaissance woman. Well done!"

The queen crowned Carmen with a bejeweled diadem to the approval of everyone in attendance. Carmen seemed thrilled with the award, yet she wore the crown with the grace befitting a lady.

Many spectators recognized Carmen from her work in the London theaters and in a few art movies, and they gossiped about stories they had heard about her in the tabloid press. The actor portraying the king signaled for quiet so he could speak.

"A Renaissance man was highly skilled in many areas, but a sharp intellect was the most valuable skill of a polymath," the king said. "The Stratford Renaissance Festival recognizes the genius of our city's greatest citizen as we proudly present your prize: *The Complete Works of William Shakespeare*."

The king handed Jon a heavy hardcover book with a color illustration of Will on the cover. He opened the book and saw there were thirty-seven plays, 154 sonnets, and several poems. Half of the plays had not been published during his life, and Jon recalled the only copies of many of the plays were hastily scribbled notes.

Jon had seen this same book in a store downtown but it cost £100. He quickly flipped through the book and read a few lines to make sure this was indeed the genuine article. Everyone began applauding as Jon read silently.

Until this moment, Jon had dreaded the idea that he might be the only person alive who remembered some of these plays, but now he knew for certain that was not the case. The plays were all here. Every one of them. Jon began to feel an immense relief and was overwhelmed with emotions.

The king and queen ushered Jon and Carmen to leave, but Jon began to speak:

"I am speechless and humbled to receive such a generous gift," Jon said. His eyes welled with tears. "Of all my worldly possessions, this is the greatest gift I could ever receive! I thank you with all my heart! I will cherish this book forever."

Several people laughed at Jon's reaction. Nearly every other person at the festival owned a copy of *The Complete Works of William Shakespeare*, and several people owned multiple versions by different publishers.

"If you have not read these plays, you must read them

at once," Jon urged. "Why are you laughing? These plays are a world treasure!"

More people laughed. Jon thought they were mocking him for expressing his emotions and grew irritated.

"We do not disagree with you about Shakespeare's greatness," the king said. "We are all happy that you like your new book. I want to thank you everyone for coming today, and I hope all of you had as much fun as we did. May you all have safe travels back to your homes, and may you keep a little piece of the past in your mind to feed your dreams."

"Fare thee well," the queen said as she waved to everyone. "Thank you and good night."

Jon and Carmen found Steve and they all walked together to the parking area where they saw Emma leaning against her Camry, dressed in the same clothes from the morning.

"Hey guys," Emma said. "How was the festival?"

"It made me feel alive for the first time in ages," Jon said. "I won all the games and contests, and I received this book as a prize."

Jon handed Emma the book.

"This is a beauty," Emma said as she inspected it. "I have a few older copies at home, but this one is top-notch. Congratulations on winning the grand prize."

"Thanks," Jon said as Emma returned his book.

"I won the women's grand prize," Carmen said and she showed Emma her diadem.

"It's lovely," Emma said. "I knew you could do it. Don't wear it under your helmet. How did you do, Steve?"

"I had fun," Steve said. "I got second place."

Everyone got inside the car. Jon traded seats with Carmen so she could sit in front with Emma, and Jon sat in the back with Steve. They all put on their seat belts.

Emma started the car and she retraced their path along the narrow roads and wide highways that wound through the green countryside.

"We looked for you everywhere," Carmen said to Emma. "Did you even go to the festival?"

"Yeah, I did the archery range and the quiz and stuff," Emma said. "I saw you three being the center of attention, but you probably didn't recognize me in my costume. The truth is, I spent most of the day with an amazing man I just met, and I know I won't be able to stop thinking about him for a long time."

"I made a new friend today too," Jon said from the back seat. He was disappointed he didn't get to see Emma but enjoyed every minute he spent with Ryan.

"Who was that pretty girl you were dancing with, Jon?" Carmen asked.

"Oh, Carmen and I had the first dance together," Jon said to Emma. "You are an excellent dancer, Carmen."

"So are you, but that's not who I meant," she said.

"She means that blonde girl from the archery range who bravely asked me to dance while you two were on your second round," Steve said. "Before she cut in."

"Who?" Emma asked.

Emma tried to watch Carmen's reaction, glance into the rearview mirror to watch Jon and Steve, and keep the car on the road.

"Jon danced with her for two dances," Carmen said.

"Her name is Alice," Jon said. "She's in high school and lives with her parents. Thanks for introducing us. You can be the maid of honor at our wedding."

Everyone laughed and then Carmen laughed with an embarrassing snort that made everyone laugh again.

They talked about the festival and their favorite costumes for a while, and then everyone sat in silence for a few minutes and stared out the windows as they drove along the highway. Jon flipped through his book for a few minutes but chose to enjoy the view instead.

"How are you doing back there, Jon?" Emma asked.

"I feel more comfortable in the back seat," Jon said. "You are an excellent driver. Thank you for driving me."

"Yeah, thanks, Emma," Carmen said.

"Thanks, Emma," Steve echoed.

"It's my pleasure, guys," Emma said. "I have to drive the Camry once in a while and it's good to leave the city."

Jon remembered the twenty-pound note Steve lent him earlier. He took the bill out of his inner pocket and held it out to Steve, discreetly so the women couldn't see.

"I didn't have an occasion to spend this but I would be grateful to borrow it for the weekend," Jon said to Steve in a lowered voice.

"You can keep it," Steve said.

"Thank you," Jon said. He put the folded bill back in his inner pocket. He looked out the window for a few minutes in silence until he had a question. He opened his book to the section for *Twelfth Night; Or, What You Will.* Jon skipped to the end of the play and read the last scene again, then turned to Steve and asked him a question.

"At the end of *Twelfth Night*, why do you think your character Duke Orsino marries Viola, after everything that just happened?" Jon asked.

Steve thought in silence for a while before answering.

"Probably so there would be a happy ending," Steve said. "I have no idea. I could never forgive a woman for something like that."

The rest of the car ride was silent until they reached London and Emma dropped everyone off at the Globe theater in Southwark. There had been a different play performed at the theater that day but it was already over and everyone was gone. Jon, Steve, and Carmen changed out of their costumes and into their own clothes. Everyone said goodbye again.

Steve and Carmen put on their helmets and they sped away on Steve's motorcycle. Jon stayed outside while Emma locked up the theater so she wouldn't be alone.

"Can I give you a lift home?" Emma asked when she had finished securing the theater.

A flood of conflicting thoughts overwhelmed Jon for a moment. He wanted to spend more time with Emma but didn't wish to ride in an automobile again.

The word "home" was painful for Jon to hear and it reminded him he had no home to call his own. He couldn't let Emma know he was sleeping in a homeless shelter and couldn't accept any more of her help until he paid her back for everything she had done for him thus far. He wanted to have a home and a family someday, but he needed more stability before such a life was possible. For now, Jon would just try to be a good friend.

"If it wasn't such a lovely evening for a walk, I might accept your offer," Jon said. "Please accept my gratitude once again for driving me to my hometown and returning me here the same day. I had a wonderful time once I got into the spirit of things. My single regret is not having the opportunity to dance with you at the end of the festival."

"Next time," Emma said. She gave Jon a warm hug. "Enjoy the rest of your weekend. See you at auditions on Monday morning."

"Do you know which play they are doing?" Jon asked.

"*Henry VIII*," Emma said.

Jon thought fate must be pulling him along this familiar path for a reason.

"Looks like I have a play to study," he said as he held up his prized possession. "I hope you enjoy the rest of your weekend as much as I will."

They departed the theater as friends.

Chapter Nine

There was a queue outside Shakespeare's Globe on Monday morning when Jon arrived. He walked to the back of the line and confirmed with the last person that it was the right place for auditions.

By the time Jon made it to the front of the queue, there were more people standing behind him. There was a sign with a drawing of a smartphone with a red "X" crossing out the phone. A corresponding message asked people to please turn off their smartphones inside the theater. He didn't have a smartphone.

When it was his turn, Jon recognized the same porter from the box office. Reece was wearing a different shirt, but otherwise was dressed the same as on Friday.

"Name?"

"Jon Henry," he said.

"You're not on the list," Reece said after double checking a few pages attached to a clipboard. "Did you receive an invitation?"

"Informally," Jon said. "I heard about it."

"We like to ask actors to submit their headshots and curriculum vitae by e-mail first, then they are invited to audition by online video," Reece said. "Everyone here was invited to today's in-person audition after completing this online pre-screening process."

"The only thing you said that I understood was curriculum vitae, and I'm still trying to figure that out for myself," Jon said. "I don't use computers and didn't bring any online videos with me. My friends told me about this opportunity and said I should come audition. Here I am."

"Who are your friends?" Reece asked.

Jon looked around the lobby but didn't see them.

"Steve, Carmen, and Emma," he said. "They are all actors at the Globe, and they're in the current production of *Twelfth Night*."

"I know who you mean," Reece said. "Wait here."

The porter went into the room with the actors who had already checked in and came back with Steve.

"Hey, Jon, glad you could make it," Steve said as he shook Jon's hand. "Are they giving you trouble?"

"I'm not on the list," Jon said.

"I can vouch for Jon," Steve said to the porter. "Just add him to the standby list and maybe there will be time for him once everyone else has gone."

Reece wrote Jon's name at the bottom of the list and said he could go wait with the other actors.

"Thank you again, Steve," Jon said. "I'm obliged."

"No problem," Steve said as they walked together to the waiting room. "I think you deserve a chance to prove yourself. Take your shot."

Emma and Carmen were in the waiting room and stood up to greet Jon when he came in with Steve. Both women greeted Jon with a friendly hug. The four friends talked about how much fun they had at Saturday's Renaissance festival. The director came into the waiting room and made an announcement.

"Ladies and gentlemen, thank you for coming today," the man said. He had gray hair and a gray beard that were both cut short and matched his gray suit. He wore spectacles with orange frames that matched an orange handkerchief in his breast pocket. "For those of you I have not met, my name is Larry, and I am the director for the upcoming production of Shakespeare's *Henry VIII*. This is Marsha, the play's casting director. We will try to interview everyone individually if there is enough time. We will make a decision on the final cast before lunch. There are roles for eight men and three women. You may audition for up to three roles. We are on a tight schedule. Are there any questions before we begin?"

"When will the show open?" someone asked.

"Three weeks from this Wednesday," Larry said.

All the auditioning actors stirred uncomfortably or quietly protested. Everyone but Jon thought three weeks wasn't enough time to prepare. Jon thought three weeks was too much time.

With no further questions, they called in the first actor to audition. Carmen followed Larry and Marsha to the main stage area while everyone else remained in the waiting room.

Jon passed the time talking with the other actors. Carmen came back and sent another actor in to the stage area. Eventually Steve was called, then Emma. About thirty actors auditioned during the two hours before Jon's name was finally called.

Jon walked down a hallway past the costume room he had visited on Saturday, through a door into the backstage area, and through another door onto the main stage.

The morning sun was shining in Jon's face as he walked to the front of the stage and stood on an "X" marked in tape. Larry and Marsha sat in metal folding chairs on the floor near the front of the raised stage.

"Go ahead, Jon," Larry said after he and Marsha had finished conversing.

"I would like to do a scene from act five, scene three," Jon said. "Archbishop Cranmer's trial. I will be doing Cranmer opposite Bishop Gardiner."

"Do you have a script?" Larry asked.

"I looked at the play yesterday, so it's still fresh in my mind," Jon said. "This is right after the council sentences Cranmer to the Tower."

Jon imagined he had been falsely accused of a crime without evidence and ordered to go to prison indefinitely. These might be his last words, but Cranmer knew more than his accusers.

"Is there no other way of mercy, but I must needs to the Tower, my lords?" Jon recited from memory.

"What other would you expect?" Larry said as he read the part for Bishop Gardiner. "You are strangely troublesome. Let some of the guard be ready there."

"For me? Must I go like a traitor thither?" Jon asked as though he could still choose not to go.

"Receive him, and see him safe in the Tower."

"Stay, good my lords, I have a little yet to say," Jon

said. A sly smile crossed his face. He held out his left hand, palm down, to show off an imaginary ring on his finger. "Look there, my lords; by virtue of that ring, I take my cause out of the gripes of cruel men, and give it to a most noble judge, the king my master."

"Good," Larry said. "Say that last part again, starting with 'stay, my good lords,' only this time, I want you to say it like you're the one sentencing Gardiner. Pretend the ring is on your middle finger and hold it up at the end. Whenever you're ready."

Jon thought about how Cranmer, the Archbishop of Canterbury, was sent to the privy council by Henry while Anne was in labor, but Cranmer was initially denied entrance. Once they allowed him inside, the council of bishops accused Cranmer of treason and heresy, stripped him of his title, and ordered him to the Tower without a fair trial. Fortunately, Cranmer had come prepared.

"Stay, good my lords, I have a little yet to say. Look there, my lords," Jon said defiantly. He held out his left fist and extended his middle finger. "By virtue of that ring, I take my cause out of the gripes of cruel men and give it to a most noble judge, the king my master."

With his imaginary ring still displayed, Jon rolled his hand to the left so his middle finger stuck up in the air as a final, rude gesture.

"Yes!" Larry shouted and clapped his hands with excitement. "Anything else?"

"Next, I would like to do act two, scene three," Jon said. "I will play Anne Boleyn opposite the old lady and Lord Chamberlin."

Larry and Marsha looked at each other curiously and then flipped through the script to the scene.

Jon's character Anne acted shocked by the thought of anyone replacing Queen Catherine.

"I swear again, I would not be a queen for all the world," Jon said without consulting a script.

"In faith, for little England you'd venture an emballing," Marsha said, reading the part of the old lady. "I myself would for Caernarvonshire, although there longed no more to the crown but that. Lo, who comes here?"

"Enter Chamberlin," Larry read, then continued, "Good morrow, ladies. What were it worth to know the secret of your conference?"

"My good lord, not your demand; it values not your asking: Our mistress' sorrows we were pitying," Jon said.

"It was a gentle business, and becoming the action of good women: there is hope all will be well," Larry read.

"Now, I pray God, amen!" Jon cried.

"You bear a gentle mind, and heavenly blessings follow such creatures," Larry read. "That you may, fair lady, perceive I speak sincerely, and high notes taken of your many virtues, the king's majesty commends his good opinion of you, and does purpose honor to you no less flowing than Marchioness of Pembroke: to which title a thousand pound a year, annual support, out of his grace he adds."

Jon imagined suddenly being granted a title with land and income. How would he react to such a life-changing gift? With humility and gratitude, he decided.

"I do not know what kind of my obedience I should tender," Jon said aside. "More than my all is nothing: nor my prayers are not words duly hallowed, nor my wishes more worth than empty vanities; yet prayers and wishes are all I can return." Jon addressed an imaginary Chamberlin character with his hands clasped together. "Beseech your lordship, vouchsafe to speak my thanks and my obedience, as from a blushing handmaid, to his highness; whose health and royalty I pray for."

"That was good," Larry said. "Do that last part again, but say it like Catherine is history and you know you will be the next queen."

Jon repeated Anne's last few lines as directed, with a noble authority, confidence, and graceful elegance.

Larry and Marsha conferred after Jon finished the scene, and then Marsha spoke.

"You seem to know this play pretty well, Jon," she said. "We want you to read another part, if that's OK."

"I'm happy to oblige," Jon said. "Which part?"

"Let's go back to act five, scene three," Marsha said as she flipped through her script. "King Henry has just come into the council and his suspicions of their corruption have been confirmed. He begins, 'You were ever good.'"

"You were ever good at sudden commendations, Bishop of Winchester," Jon said in a deep and powerful voice as he slowly circled an imaginary character on stage. The king was irritated and wanted answers. "But know, I come not to hear such flattery now, and in my presence; they are too thin and bare to hide offenses. To me you cannot reach, you play the spaniel, and think with wagging of your tongue to win me; but, whatsoever thou takest me for, I'm sure thou hast a cruel nature and a bloody."

Jon looked over to where Cranmer would be standing on stage and addressed the imaginary character.

"Good man, sit down," Jon continued as King Henry. "Now let me see the proudest he, that dares most, but wag his finger at thee. By all that's holy, he had better starve than but once think this place becomes thee not."

"May it please your grace," Marsha read.

"No, sir, it does not please me!" King Henry shouted. "I had thought I had had men of some understanding and wisdom of my council; but I find none. Was it discretion, lords, to let this man, this good man – few of you deserve that title – this honest man, wait like a lousy footboy at chamber door? And one as great as you are? Why, what a shame was this!" The king was furious at the council and felt he couldn't trust anyone. "Did my commission bid ye so far forget yourselves? I gave ye power as he was a counselor to try him, not as a groom. There's some of ye, I see, more out of malice than integrity, would try him to the utmost, had ye mean – which ye shall never have while I live."

Jon waited for Larry or Marsha to read the next line but they just looked at him in awe. After a moment of speechlessness, they conferred with each other again for what seemed to Jon to be at least two minutes.

"We don't have any information about you, Jon," Larry said. "Where have you worked? How long have you been doing Shakespeare? How do you know *Henry VIII*?"

"*Henry VIII* was the most recent play in which I acted," Jon said. "I played Anne Boleyn. I studied theater and music at a children's abbey in London and I began acting at the new Globe Theater in 1600. I've done every play by Shakespeare in my thirteen-year career. I once received a special commendation from her majesty Queen Elizabeth for my portrayal of Viola in *Twelfth Night*."

"Did you say in 1600?" Marsha asked.

"Did I?" Jon asked. "Yes."

"That would be Elizabeth I, then, not Elizabeth II," Marsha said. "You seem like a true believer, Jon."

"Who's your agent?" Larry asked. "Are you in an actor's union?"

"No. I will need help with all that," Jon said.

Larry and Marsha conferred privately for another few minutes before they told Jon he could go.

"Marsha and I need to discuss some changes," Larry said. "Don't send anyone else in, and don't go home yet."

Jon went through the backstage and down the hallway to the waiting room.

"How did it go, Jon?" Emma asked.

"I thought it went well, but I never know with auditions," he said. "I did my best."

"That's what matters most," Steve said. "Always do your best and live your life with no regrets. You'll never get what you want if you don't try."

Noon came and went and the directors continued to deliberate their final decision. At a quarter to one, the directors came back to the waiting room.

"Thank you everyone for waiting so patiently," Larry

said. "Marsha and I thought we had the play cast, until our Henry came in. He changed our minds and we had to rethink the cast."

Larry read the names of the parts and the actors who would be playing them. Many of the minor roles were combined so one actor had up to three different roles.

Carmen got the role of Catherine of Aragon. Larry listed the actors who would be playing the roles of Cardinal Wolsey, the Duke of Buckingham, and Lord Sands. When he announced Steve would play the role of Lord Chamberlin in addition to Archbishop Cranmer and an unnamed secretary to the cardinal, Jon began to worry he might not get a role.

Jon believed it was his destiny to portray Anne Boleyn again and deliver her controversial farewell monologue. Thus, he was surprised when Emma was chosen to be the next Anne Boleyn and not he. Jon was happy for all his friends and congratulated them.

Larry got through all the supporting roles and then announced the big change: Jon would play the title role of King Henry VIII. Steve would be Jon's understudy.

Larry and Marsha thanked everyone for auditioning and said the Globe would hold auditions for their next play on the same day next month. Rehearsals were scheduled to begin after dinner, and everyone who didn't get a part was asked to leave. When the last of the audition losers left, the caterers carried in several platters of sandwiches, fresh fruit slices, and an assortment of snacks.

Jon had not expected auditions to take so long, and he had not yet eaten. When he inquired about the cost of the meals, he was told dinner was a free perk during rehearsals so actors could work all day without leaving the theater. Jon had two sandwiches and some fruit. After everyone had eaten, he grabbed some leftover sandwiches to have for his supper.

The actors set up a dozen chairs in a circle facing in. Each actor took a seat, and Larry had the twelfth seat. Larry introduced himself, and the actors took turns introducing themselves with their names, where they were trained, favorite parts they played on stage, other actors they worked with, their style of acting, and their hopes for their future career. Most of the actors had worked together previously on a production, seen each other in a play, or knew of each other.

Carmen said she was from Toledo, Spain, and Steve said he was from somewhere called Brooklyn in New York City. Jon had no idea where that was.

Jon stood up to speak when it was his turn.

"My name is Jon Henry," he began. "Most of you don't know me and I don't know you, but I hope we will correct that soon. Verily, I didn't know this place existed a week ago. I saw a play on Friday night, came back twice on Saturday, and now this is my fourth time inside in as many days. This place is a dream to me and today my dreams have come true."

"Where were you before a week ago?" Larry asked.

"I studied music and theater at an all-boys school in London when I was thirteen, and I began acting professionally when I turned eighteen," Jon said. "I started here at the Globe when it was first built, and for thirteen years thereafter. My favorite roles to play were Viola, Lady Macbeth, Cleopatra, Beatrice, and Rosalind because they had the courage to stand up for what they wanted. I've never played the lead before but I'm hungry for the opportunity. I loathe being out of work and it feels like it's been four hundred years since my last role."

"Would you consider your acting style to be classical or method?" Emma asked.

"What is the difference?" Jon asked.

"Classical acting is memorizing every word and perfecting your costume, voice, and movements to be as precise and authentic as possible," Emma said. "Method acting is looking like, behaving like, and experiencing the same emotions as your character, sometimes off stage."

Most of the roles Jon had played were women. He wondered whether Emma was asking if he ever dressed and behaved like a woman when he was not acting on stage or if she meant becoming a tyrant while playing one.

"You mean like ordering my wife to be beheaded?" Jon joked. "I may be eccentric, but I'm not crazy."

"I mean like living off the grid with no computers or modern technology," Emma said. "Changing how you speak and act to stay true to the character you're playing."

"Can an actor be both types?" Jon asked.

"Yes, there are many different approaches that can work and it's a matter of personal preference," Larry said. "Jon, how and where did you learn to do the original pronunciation of Renaissance words?"

"I don't understand your question," Jon said. "This is how I speak."

"Modern vowel sounds are much different," Larry said. "You speak like they did in Shakespeare's time."

"Do I?" Jon asked. "In Shakespeare's time? How could you know that?"

"I have a master's degree in linguistics," Larry said. "I have been in theater for more than twenty years, and in all that time, I have never …" Larry stopped himself. "I will save that story for another time. Jon. Last question: What are your hopes for your future career?"

Jon thought for a moment.

"To be honest, I've thought about my past a lot more than I've thought about my future," he said. "Every time I come in here, I feel like it's 1613. By the time we start doing performances, I'll probably fancy it's 1530 again. My hopes are to be able to keep acting for a long time. This is the greatest job in the world and it's the only work I've ever known. It's an honor to be your king, and I hope we all become good friends in the future."

The actors finished introductions and then read the play *Henry VIII* from the beginning. Each actor had their own script with their character's lines highlighted. They read their own parts and spoke at the speed of a normal conversation. It took approximately three hours to read through to the ending.

When they had finished, Larry asked if there were any more questions before they quit for the day.

"I would like to know what the hell happened to the ending," Jon said. No one knew what he meant. "Scene four of act five should be Anne's farewell speech, but it's missing entirely. The ending is all wrong."

"We did not change the ending," Larry said. "This script is straight from the *First Folio*, published in 1623."

"It's the same in my own copy," Jon said. "It must be called *The Complete Works* because this ending is complete bollocks! Even the title of the play is different. I want to know who butchered this ending!"

"*Henry VIII* was co-authored by John Fletcher," Larry recalled.

"Fletcher!" Jon cursed. "Of course! I know he's behind this. Fletch was against doing the scene. He was afraid the audience would riot."

"Which scene was that?" Larry asked. "You said act five, scene four?" He flipped to the last few pages of the script. The ten other cast members also flipped through their scripts. "I don't see anything here. What was her farewell speech that was cut?"

Jon recited Anne's last words in his normal voice instead of his woman's voice. As he was saying her words, he imagined the last time he spoke them. Jon was crossing the street with Will when a horse and cart nearly trampled them both. Anne's last words were almost Jon's last words. Tears welled in Jon's eyes as he spoke her final prayers with a tenderness that moved Larry and a few of the cast members.

"Well, that's certainly a much more powerful ending," Larry said. He removed the orange handkerchief from his breast pocket, cleaned his glasses, and wiped his nose. Larry replaced his glasses and his handkerchief. "What was Fletcher's objection?"

"People were infuriated by the injustice done to

Anne," Jon said. "It was incredible. Everyone spoke of the ending like they couldn't believe it was true. I was in favor of keeping the true ending, and I still am."

When they had finished their discussion, some of the cast members made plans to meet at Ganymede's pub for a drink. Jon was planning to go there anyway so he went along with everyone.

Ganymede's was much less crowded on Monday night compared to Friday. Most of the tables were empty and the barstools were just beginning to fill up. Jon didn't see Ryan. Everyone ordered drinks except for Jon.

"We have been paired together again," Carmen said to Jon while Steve was getting another drink from the bartender. "Why do you think this keeps happening?"

"Surely it was meant to be, milady Greensleeves," Jon said playfully. "Henry and Catherine didn't choose each other, at first."

"They didn't?" Emma asked.

"No," Jon continued in a lowered tone that suggested confidence. Carmen and Emma leaned in closer to hear Jon better. "Catherine was married to Henry's older brother Prince Arthur when they were children. Arthur and Catherine both got sick, and he died before they could consummate the marriage. Prince Henry's father – King Henry VII – considered marrying Catherine himself to collect the rest of her dowry but decided against it. When Henry VII died, Henry VIII became the king, and married his brother's widow, the princess dowager. Catherine was five years older than Henry."

"A younger man and an older woman? That sounds

like you, Emma," Carmen joked.

"All of Henry's other five wives were much younger than him," Jon said. "Catherine Howard was not yet twenty years when they married, and Henry was fifty."

"That's just gross," Emma said.

"She also lost her head," Jon said.

Steve came over with a small glass of amber liquid.

"This is an eighteen-year-old, single-malt Scotch whisky," Steve said as he handed the drink to Jon.

"Why, thank you," Jon said. He examined the drink and smelled it. "Aqua vitae. The water of life."

"Long live the new King Henry, our dread sovereign," Steve said as he raised his own glass to Jon.

All the other cast members in the bar raised their glasses to Jon as well. Jon smiled and raised his glass to accept the toast.

"God save the king!" Jon shouted.

"God save the king!" everyone repeated. They drank their beverages, but Jon did not.

Steve noticed Jon had not had any of his drink.

"You don't drink Scotch?" Steve asked.

"I swore off drinking alcohol, and I can't break an oath to myself," Jon said. "Sorry. You can have it."

"You don't drink?" Steve repeated. "I had no idea. I'm sorry I put you on the spot like that. But what are you doing in a pub if you're not drinking or eating?"

"You guys are my friends," Jon said. "I'd rather be here than anywhere else right now. And I'm waiting to meet with another friend."

"That guy you met in Stratford?" Emma asked.

"His name is Ryan," Jon said. "I think you guys would like him. We made plans to meet today after five o'clock. What time is it now?"

"It's a quarter past five," Steve said.

"Speaking of mysterious men, have you heard back from that guy you met on Saturday?" Carmen asked.

"Not yet, but it's only been two days," Emma said. "I need to get going. I'll see you guys tomorrow. This is going to be a great show."

Everyone said goodbye to Emma as she left.

"Hey, what was that business today about Fletcher and an alternate ending?" Steve asked.

"I remember this play had a better ending," Jon said. "It still feels fresh in my mind. It was definitely more provocative than the printed version, and it was the truth."

"Anne Boleyn's farewell speech was beautiful," Carmen said. "I keep thinking about it."

"It changed my opinion of her," Steve admitted. "Why do you think Fletcher changed the ending? Your version is way better."

"I don't know who changed it," Jon said. "It could have been lost in the fire."

As soon as Jon spoke the words, his mind went back to the afternoon of June 29, 1613. The Globe Theater was aflame. Jon and the other actors had helped the 3,000 spectators to safely exit and they were trying to save whatever costumes and props they could. Jon saved his dresses and then went back inside for Will.

"They were performing this play when the original Globe burned down," Steve said.

"He was trying to carry everything," Jon recalled. "It was too much for him to carry by himself, but he wouldn't leave anything behind. He couldn't."

Jon remembered the weight of the satchel filled with handwritten plays he had saved from the fire.

"If it wasn't destroyed by fire, it was edited out later," Steve said. "Neither one would surprise me."

Steve drank the Scotch intended for Jon.

"How did just this one part of the play go missing?" Carmen asked. "Could a single page have fallen out?"

"That's possible," Jon said. He thought it was an unlikely coincidence that the page with Anne Boleyn's farewell would be the only page to fall out during the fire. Jon and his colleagues had been talking about that same speech before the show began.

"You have a good imagination, but don't try to think too hard about it," Steve said. "Carmen and I are going to supper. We'll see you at work tomorrow, King Henry."

Jon wished his friends well and continued to drink his glass of ice water at the bar. He kept thinking about the fire and how that one page could have been removed from the rest, when he realized that he had looked at that same page just before the fire started.

Jon felt his heart sink and his anxiety rise. He had forgotten to replace the page with Anne Boleyn's final words that he had removed to study one more time.

"Hey, Shakespeare, why so sad?" asked a familiar voice. "Looks like I got here too late."

Jon looked up from his ice water and saw Ryan standing behind him. Ryan was wearing gray pants, a white dress shirt with the collar unbuttoned and the sleeves rolled up to his elbows, and a red-and-white-striped necktie, which was loosened.

"I think it's my fault," Jon said sadly.

He stood up to greet Ryan and was surprised to receive a comforting hug instead of a firm handshake. Jon returned the momentary, brotherly embrace that ended with two manly shoulder pats from each gentleman.

"Thanks. I needed that," Jon said.

"Maybe I got here just in time," Ryan said. "What's your fault?"

"I looked at the page with Anne Boleyn's final words during the performance and I forgot to replace it," Jon said as he looked at the ice cubes floating in his drink. "Then the fire started and there wasn't time to get organized. We barely got out alive."

"You started the fire?" Ryan asked.

"No," Jon said. "The cannon blast at Wolsey's party accidentally set the thatch roof on fire. I was on stage."

"Then it wasn't your fault," Ryan said.

"I didn't put the page back and now there's a vital piece of history missing from the play," Jon said. "It's only one scene, but it changes everything."

"It wasn't your fault, but it feels like it to you," Ryan said. "How can you atone for an accident?"

"By fixing the ending of *Henry VIII*," Jon said. "I feel like I have a new purpose. A lot has happened since I saw you last. How art thou?"

"Busy with work," Ryan said. "I started a new project today so I will be working double shifts three days a week.

The pay is good and I still have my weekends so I can't really complain. What are you drinking?"

"Ice water," Jon said.

"Do you want anything else?"

"I don't drink alcohol," Jon said.

Ryan signaled to the bartender and ordered two more ice waters. Even though the water was complimentary, Ryan tipped the bartender five pounds for the service.

"What's new with you?" Ryan asked.

"I won the festival on Saturday and this morning at auditions I got the lead role," Jon said. "I'm the king."

"Congratulations, your majesty," Ryan said.

"Thanks. I've never played Henry VIII before, and he sounds both fun and scary."

"What did he do that was so scary?" Ryan asked.

"He had his second wife executed for high treason after she had a miscarriage, then he married his third wife eleven days later."

"That is scary," Ryan admitted.

"I think something happened in 1536 that changed him," Jon said. "Where I can research Henry VIII?"

Ryan pulled his smartphone out of his pocket and began tapping on its flat surface.

"Henry VIII was injured in a jousting accident on January 24, 1536 that researchers think resulted in a traumatic brain injury," Ryan read. "This says his armored horse fell on top of him and he was unconscious for two hours. Henry was fully armored and suffered no other physical injuries. This article says Anne Boleyn was so distressed by the news that she herself fell and a few days later she delivered a stillborn son several months early."

"That was it," Jon said. "The catalyst for his change in behavior was this head injury."

"It looks like 1536 was a terrible year for Henry VIII," Ryan said as he continued reading his smartphone. "His first wife Catherine of Aragon died January 7, Henry fell from his horse at the Greenwich tiltyard on the twenty-fourth, and Anne suffered her miscarriage on the twenty-ninth. In March, Henry began dissolving the monasteries. Anne and her brother were arrested and executed in May and Henry married Jane Seymour, a lady in waiting to both Catherine and Anne. There were more major religious reforms that summer, and by October, tens of thousands of people rebelled against the reforms."

"None of that is in the play *Henry VIII*," Jon said. "Where did you find that information?"

"I just did a search for Henry VIII and 1536," Ryan said. "If you don't have a smartphone or a computer, you can find thousands of books written about Henry VIII at any bookstore or library."

"That's a good idea," Jon said. "I will go to a library."

"Do you want to hang out this weekend?" Ryan asked. "I'm occupied all week until Saturday morning."

"Let's meet on Saturday morning," Jon said. "They serve breakfast here. We can meet at Ganymede's at around eight or nine."

"It's a date," Ryan said. "See you Saturday morning."

The friends shook hands and parted.

Chapter Ten

Jon woke up on Saturday morning anticipating his first day off. He arrived at Ganymede's before it opened and was their first customer. Jon purchased a cup of coffee, a slice of spanakopita, and a newspaper which he read at a table next to a window.

The newspaper stories were about protests against new government regulations on something Jon didn't fully understand. He flipped through the pages and didn't see anything that looked important. There was a magazine inserted in the newspaper and Jon took it out to examine it closer. It was a current real estate and renter's guide to homes and apartments in Southwark.

He looked at the different available places and compared prices and features. The nicest apartments cost around £6 million, with great views and new appliances, plus communal activity rooms and large lobby areas. Most of the apartments rented for £1,000 a month, which was more than he could afford. The listings were grouped in confusing ways to Jon and most of the pages didn't have anything even remotely close to his price range.

"Are we apartment hunting today?" Ryan asked.

Jon looked up and saw his friend standing nearby.

Ryan was wearing a brown tweed suit with brown leather elbow patches sewn on the jacket sleeves. He wore a blue dress shirt with the collar unbuttoned, a loosened black necktie, and brown leather shoes.

Jon stood up and gave Ryan a friendly hug.

"Yesterday was pay day and I desperately need to upgrade my living arrangements," Jon said. "I looked at this guide but I can't find what I want. It's so frustrating."

"Have you looked online?" Ryan asked. Jon looked at him blankly. "Let me help." Ryan took out his smartphone and began tapping on the screen. "Here we go. How big of a place are you looking for?"

"It's just me and I don't need much."

"A studio will work," Ryan said. "Any pets?"

"No."

"Furnished or unfurnished?" Ryan asked.

"Either is fine," Jon said. "I don't have any furniture."

"What's your budget?" Ryan asked.

"About eight hundred pounds per month," Jon said.

"That narrowed the field considerably," Ryan said. "Take a look at these pictures and tell me if you want to visit any of them today." Ryan handed his smartphone to Jon, who looked at the first picture.

"Where are the other pictures?" Jon asked.

"You have to swipe your finger across the screen to go to the next image," Ryan instructed.

Jon swiped the first image like he was turning the page of a book and the image changed. He swiped again and saw another image of the same apartment from a different angle. He continued swiping until he cycled through to the first image again, then he handed the phone back to Ryan.

"See anything you like?" Ryan asked.

"Not really," Jon said. "I don't do electronics and I don't want all those fancy contraptions. I want my home to be simple and quiet; a refuge from city life. A view would also be nice. And close to the Globe."

Ryan tapped some more times to narrow the search results even further. There was one result.

"I think I found something," Ryan said and he began to read from his device. "'Fourth-floor, walk-up, spacious loft, partially furnished, no pets. View of St. Paul's. Common kitchen, laundry, and bathrooms.' It's close to here and the price is in your range. This says it became available two minutes ago. I'm going to call them."

Ryan tapped the screen once and then held the device up to his ear and stared at nothing while the call connected.

"Hi, I saw you have an apartment available," Ryan said and he briefly described the ad. "Can I come see it? In about five minutes? Great! I will meet you there in about five minutes."

Ryan tapped the screen again and set down his smartphone.

"This place looks really cute," Ryan said.

"Cute?" Jon asked.

"I mean it looks like it could serve you well as a bachelor pad," Ryan said. "Except for the stairs, it looks perfect. If you have any guests, they had better be in good shape to make it up four flights. Let's go."

Jon finished eating his spinach-filled pastry and

washed it down with the rest of his coffee.

"I don't mind the stairs," Jon said. "The top floor has the best view."

They walked a few blocks to the four-story building marked on Ryan's smartphone. The building was constructed in 1950 and it was recently retrofitted for electricity, plumbing, and had an emergency fire sprinkler system. A man was standing outside the building when they arrived.

The man wore a denim vest over a black T-shirt and denim jeans. His arms were covered with menacing tattoos. He had a gray goatee and long, gray hair that was tied in a ponytail.

"We're here to look at the apartment," Ryan said to the man.

"Both of you?" the man asked.

"Just me," Jon said. "He helped me find you."

"I listed the apartment minutes ago and you are the first to see it," he said. "I hope you like stairs."

"How else would you get to the top?" Jon asked. "Climb a ladder?"

"He means there's no lift," Ryan said.

"What's a lift?" Jon asked.

"I like this guy," the man said. "Fourth floor."

The man began climbing the stairs one at a time and kept one hand steadied by the handrail. Jon and Ryan followed a few steps behind. The man's pace slowed after the second floor, and he had to sit down on a bench at the top to catch his breath.

He stood up after a minute and walked to the middle

door. The man checked his pockets and then cursed to himself. He checked all his jacket pockets, then rechecked his pants pockets. The man cursed again. He looked down the stairs and back at the door. He tried the door handle and it was unlocked.

"Come inside and see the apartment," the man said as he wiped the sweat from his forehead. He went inside and the two men followed him in.

The apartment had large windows with a stunning view of London and St. Paul's Cathedral across the river Thames. There was a sink and cupboard in one corner and electrical outlets for a small refrigerator and microwave. The floors were polished, hardwood oak and only a little squeaky. Everything was clean and shiny.

There was a queen-sized mattress on the floor opposite the sink area, but no other furniture or appliances. Jon tested the mattress and it seemed comfortable and didn't smell bad.

"There's a bathroom and shower on every floor but this one," the man said. "Kitchen area is on the ground floor. Everyone has their own food cupboard in the kitchen, which makes food ownership less contentious. Laundry is in the basement."

"I like it," Jon said. "How much?"

The man told Jon the monthly rate, plus deposit. Jon paid the man most of the cash he received the day before. He had enough, but was broke again until the next payday.

"What do you do for a living?" the man asked.

"I'm an actor at Shakespeare's Globe," Jon said.

"Ah, Shakespeare," the man said. "To be or not to be.

Try not to be too loud, especially late at night. There's a family living below you on the third floor. Most of the other residents are college students, actors, or immigrant workers. Rent is due on the first of every month. Don't be late. Let's go back down to the office and I will get you keys and a rental agreement."

Jon didn't have photo identification but that wasn't a problem. Ryan helped Jon complete the paperwork and Jon got the keys to his new apartment.

"You got lucky with this place," Ryan said. "Do you need help moving any boxes or furniture?"

"This is all I have, other than my book and a few other belongings I have in a locker," Jon said. "I might need some house things like a table and some chairs."

"And a couch for guests," Ryan said. "Wait; you don't have any stuff? Where were you living?"

"I've been sleeping at a shelter next to Southwark Cathedral," Jon admitted.

"You were homeless?" Ryan asked. His eyes welled with tears. Ryan looked away and dabbed his eyes on a blue handkerchief from his breast pocket. "I had no idea."

"I have a home now," Jon said. "And it's thanks to you, Ryan."

Jon extended his hand to shake Ryan's but Ryan gave him a hug instead. The friendly embrace ended with multiple back pats and then the men stepped apart again.

"Let's go find you some furniture," Ryan said.

They returned to the street and walked to the nearby Borough Market to look for supplies. The street was covered with an enormous green, metal-framed Victorian arcade. Beneath the glass arcade were dozens of individual vendor booths on either side selling wholesale fruits and vegetables, fresh bread, meats, cheeses, and a wide variety of pastries. People were walking around, shopping, talking with friends, or watching other people.

"Will and I used to come here," Jon said. "I love the new ceiling. It looks great and you can shop in the rain."

Ryan looked at the green, metal-and-glass arcade.

"This roof was built in the mid-nineteenth century," Ryan said.

"Well, it still looks new," Jon said.

Jon purchased some fresh fruits and vegetables, a loaf of fresh sourdough bread, and a packet of paper plates, cups, and plastic utensils.

"I found a free table and chairs," Ryan said. "It's on our way and if we leave now, we might get it."

Ryan and Jon followed the directions on Ryan's smartphone to an address where there was a used table and chairs stacked on the side of the road for garbage collection. The men arranged the chairs and groceries to balance on top of the inverted table and they carried everything to Jon's apartment building.

The men stopped to remove their tweed jackets and vests and rolled up their shirt sleeves. They placed their clothes on the pile and carried it inside the lobby. Next, they carefully carried the pile up the four flights of stairs, with Ryan guiding the top and walking upstairs backwards and Jon at the bottom, bearing most of the weight.

Jon put his food away in the cupboard while Ryan set up the table and chairs. Jon sat on the bed and looked at the newspaper's classified ads.

"I still need a couch," he said. "Preferably free."

Ryan finished arranging the chairs and then turned one to face Jon and sat down. He took out his smartphone.

"Let me look," Ryan said. "Are you allergic to dogs? Never mind. Here's one that belonged to parents of a toddler. Yuck. Here's one that some cat evidently loved. Ooh! I think you're going to like this one."

Ryan showed Jon his smartphone, which pictured a two-seat black leather couch.

"Yes," Jon said. "Where is it?"

Ryan looked at his phone and stood up.

"Three blocks from here. It's free so we need to hurry. Remember to lock the door."

Jon locked the door and they hurried down the stairs, taking two or three stairs with every step. They got to the bottom and Ryan kept running so Jon ran next to him. They raced each other to the end of the street and stopped for a red traffic light.

"I won," Jon said. He was out of breath.

"You always win," Ryan said, also out of breath.

The light changed to green and they crossed the street.

"I see the couch," Jon said, and he resumed running. Ryan also ran and they reached the couch at the same time.

The men caught their breath by sitting on the couch, which they found to be clean and comfortable. Jon noticed some people approaching so he and Ryan picked up the couch and carried it in the direction from which they came. The other people also wanted the couch but they didn't follow it to Jon's apartment.

When they arrived back at Jon's building, they set down the couch and took another short rest before their ascent up the stairs. The leather couch was heavy but they made it to the top. Jon unlocked the door and they moved the couch inside so it sat next to the windows.

"Lucky, lucky, and lucky," Ryan said as he relaxed on the new couch and stared out the window at London.

"I'm lucky you know how to use that smartphone," Jon said. He removed two paper cups from the package and filled them with water from the sink tap. "You and I make a good team." Jon handed one of the cups of water to Ryan.

"Thanks," Ryan said. "There's more room here than I thought. You should consider getting a roommate."

"Why do I need a roommate?" Jon asked.

"To help share the bills, share the housework, and for companionship."

"You should be my roommate," Jon said. "You can have the couch or the bed."

"I, um, I think that would be, um, great, but currently impossible," Ryan stammered. His face was bright red. "I still have a few months on my lease and I can't leave without giving my roommate adequate notice."

"Well, my offer stands if you change your mind," Jon said. "I don't want anyone else to be my roommate."

"What about a girlfriend?" Ryan asked. "Now that you have a job and an apartment, you need a girlfriend."

"Do I?" Jon asked.

Ryan took out his smartphone and began tapping on the screen with both thumbs.

"You're way too hot to be single," he said. "What's your type, Jon?"

"Someone single, who has a sense of humor and good taste in art and culture," Jon said. "I like women who like me for who I am, not for some role I've played."

Ryan showed Jon his phone with a picture of a woman's smiling face, her first name and her interests.

"Just swipe to see the next person," Ryan said.

"Who are these people?" Jon asked as he swiped.

"Single ladies who live in the greater London area," Ryan said.

"These are ladies of easy virtue?" Jon asked.

"I hope not," Ryan said. "It's not that type of dating site. You just pick someone who looks good, say hello, and see where it leads. You can narrow your search by selecting desired physical attributes like age, height, weight, and hair color, along with income, education, and religion, if those things are important to you in a partner."

"Sounds just like apartment hunting," Jon said. "You can narrow the search until you find something you like. It helps to know what you like and what you can afford."

"This is different from apartment hunting because it's for dating," Ryan said. "If you're interested, you have to enter your own information and post a picture on their website so single ladies can look at your profile and decide if they want to go out with you."

"Still sounds like apartment hunting," Jon said. "You can keep trying out new ladies until you get lucky."

"Some people use it like that," Ryan said. "They always have way more men than women on these sites so a lot of women will filter out potential matches who are short or who report lower education and income levels. The problem is that some men are liars who pretend to be something they're not and they might look like the perfect guy online and turn out to be a real loser in person."

"Do you have a profile on there?" Jon asked.

"Um, no. I have a problem with trusting strangers who look too good to be true," Ryan said.

"I know what you mean," Jon said. "Do you know of any single ladies who aren't liars, losers, or bawds? I would prefer an introduction from a friend to dating a total stranger. Someone you think I might like."

"I believe you know my sister, Emma Morgan."

"Emma is your sister?" Jon asked. "She said she's seeing someone she met in Stratford-upon-Avon and they were taking it slowly. I want someone single."

"Trust me, that Stratford guy is nothing to worry about," Ryan said.

"I only have one rule and that's to never date my fans or my fellow actors," Jon said. "Women can be actors now so perhaps that rule is outdated. I don't know your sister very well and I sincerely mean her no disrespect, but actors are emotionally fragile and unpredictable people who will do anything for praise should they cease to be the focus of attention. A beautiful and talented woman like Emma could pretend to be anything or anyone in order to get what she wanted. These are great attributes for an actor but not for a normal human being. It's crucial to the sanity of an actor to know who they really are when the costumes and makeup come off. Otherwise, their whole life is just an act. Their whole life is a lie."

"You really think Emma is beautiful and talented?"

"She is absolutely stunning," Jon said. "A goddess."

"When I told Emma you and I were hanging out, she said she likes you but tried to be friendly to you several times and each time you rejected her," Ryan said.

"I suppose she isn't used to rejection," Jon said.

"Usually she's the one rejecting all the men trying to take her to bed," Ryan said.

"That's what I assumed," Jon said. "Lots of suitors. I'm surprised she isn't married. How old is she?"

"She would not want me to say," Ryan said.

"Well, how old art thou then?" Jon asked.

"The same age as my sister," Ryan said. "We are twins. Pray tell, how old art thou?"

"I am thirty," Jon said. "Emma was very friendly at our first meeting and she offered to buy me a drink." Ryan didn't seem to understand so Jon tried to be more direct. "Actors have a reputation for being easy to take to bed."

"Emma is not like that," Ryan said. "I can vouch for her good character. I think if you knew her better, you would find her to be your equal in many respects."

"I apologize for my mistaken assumption, and I will give her another chance, with your blessing, of course."

"If you make her happy I will be happy, and if you make her unhappy, I will be unhappy," Ryan said.

"I would like to ask your sister out on a proper date," Jon said. "What should I say? Where should we go? What does she like to do for fun? What's her favorite food?"

"Slow down, Romeo," Ryan said. "You should find

that out on your date with her, not from me. I think you should tell her how you really feel."

"I will tell her that her generous heart has given my own heart a new rhythm," Jon said. "I shall let her know I picture her face so often in my dreams that I cannot know for sure if I am sleeping or awake until I see her face at work in the morning. Emma sees the world with genuine kindness and beauty. When I stare into her azure eyes, I feel so at home and at peace that nothing else is even worth seeing."

"That sounds wonderful, but I don't think she will believe it," Ryan said. "You don't look like you're in love with anyone but yourself."

"Counterfeit, I assure you," Jon said. "Your words have given me hope for love where before I had none. My tender heart is reborn and my whole world has improved. I wish you could share my happiness. What about thou? Are there any beauties who hold the key to your heart?"

"I'm not as lucky with the ladies as you might think," he said. "Women don't exactly throw themselves at me like they do for you."

"Women throw themselves at me?" Jon asked.

"Didn't you notice all those ladies staring at you in Stratford?" Ryan asked. "I heard all the pretty women wanted to dance with you. No one even looked at me."

"I thought they were admiring my doublet," Jon said. "Verily, I was looking for your sister most of the time and I paid them little attention. If you're trying to catch the eyes of a lady you need to do something to set yourself apart from the others. You have a very pleasant face. Do the ladies admire your beard and mustache?"

"Not particularly," Ryan said. "Neither do I."

"Then why have it?" Jon asked. "Your nose and cheekbones are handsome. I bet you have a striking face."

"I like the appearance of facial hair," Ryan said. "A strong beard does not make a strong man, but I look like a woman without one."

"They say a beard does not make a philosopher," Jon said. "My friend Steve has a beard, and he has a beautiful girlfriend, so maybe you should grow your beard out like Steve's. I will need to have a full beard to play Henry, but I haven't shaved since I got the part and I doubt it will grow to fullness before the play opens."

"You should use spirit gum to stick a false beard to your face," Ryan said. He handed Jon a small bottle he had in his pocket.

"Is this what you use?" Jon joked.

"What? This is my real beard," Ryan said.

"Your beard looks unchanged every time I see you," Jon said. "I'm just being facetious. I like your beard."

"Thanks," Ryan said. "It's a reflection of my sense of style. If someone can't see past a little facial hair to find out what I'm like as a person, they've already decided they're not going to be my friend."

"You're my friend with or without the beard," Jon said. "If Emma asks about me, please put in a good word."

"You can count on it," Ryan said.

* * *

All the actors were off book at the next rehearsal on Monday morning and did not need their scripts. Jon began assembling a sandwich during the break and Emma started building her own on the opposite side of the table.

"I heard you moved into a new place last weekend," Emma said. "How are you settling in?"

"Very modestly," Jon said. "It still needs a lot of work. Ryan was a huge help. Thanks for asking."

They both finished assembling their sandwiches.

"Would you do me the honor of accompanying me to dinner sometime?" Jon asked. "Not at the Globe."

"I would like that," Emma said. "This week is crazy busy every day but I am available on Saturday."

"Saturday is great," Jon said. "When and where do you want to meet?"

Emma wrote her address on a piece of paper and handed it to Jon. Her note said "2 p.m. Saturday."

They continued rehearsals, and for the rest of the week, Jon and Emma were friendly and flirtatious with each other in their conversations offstage.

* * *

On Saturday afternoon, Jon checked the time on a public clock and then returned to the street corner where he had walked Emma home on the first night they met. He read the address Emma wrote and looked at the street names and numbers on the houses until he found her house. Her front door had a natural oak color with three diamond-shaped windows on the top. Jon pressed the button to ring the doorbell.

Emma opened the door a few moments later wearing a cute yellow dress and matching shoes. She was smiling.

"You look better than these flowers," Jon said as he

revealed a dozen yellow roses he had hidden behind his back. "I should have gone with red."

"No, they're perfect," Emma said. Jon handed the flowers to Emma and she accepted them. "Thank you! I need to put these in some water. Do you mind waiting out here for a few minutes? My place is kind of a mess."

Emma went inside her apartment and came out again a few minutes later. She gave Jon a hug and kissed him on his cheek.

"That's for the flowers," she said with a smile. "Where are we going?"

"I thought we could walk and talk, maybe to a restaurant," he said. "Are you OK to walk in those shoes?"

"These are good for walking," she said.

Jon and Emma could see the Shard, London Bridge, and Southwark Cathedral ahead as they walked north to Borough Market.

"Ryan and I were here last weekend," Jon said when they arrived. "He was such a huge help. He'd tap on his device and have an answer to any question. He was incredible. Ryan seems like more of a Renaissance man than I am."

"You should see him without his smartphone," she said. "He's not so smart."

"I met him at the Renaissance fair and he didn't have his smartphone," Jon said. "Ryan has a sense of beauty and grace that's rare for a gentleman. You probably know why he's still single. It's none of my business."

"Do you have any romantic feelings for my brother?" Emma asked. "Your admiration seems mutual."

"It's more like a fellowship or brotherhood," Jon said. "It feels good to have a friend who understands me. I feel comfortable when I'm around him. No offense intended, but I don't think I could ever have a relationship with a woman like my friendship with Ryan."

"That does not sound romantic as you describe it but it does sound fulfilling," Emma said. "My closest female friend is my mum, but she was already a mother when she was my age. Most of my friends are not parents yet. In any conversation with my mum, there is a subconscious pressure to find a man, marry, and have babies."

"I haven't felt that pressure you call subconscious," Jon said. "I never had any children."

"Would you want to have children some day in the future?" Emma asked. "That's a fair question for a first date. I need to know if you are dad material or just another handsome stud who's passing through."

"It would be a great blessing if it happened and I would change my entire life," Jon said.

"Great answer."

"How about you?" Jon asked. "Do you have any children? You said it's a fair question."

"No, I don't have any children," Emma said.

"Are you starting to feel that subconscious pressure to meet a man, marry, and have babies?" Jon asked.

"Yes," Emma said. "Subconsciously."

"When I was portraying Anne Boleyn, especially during her final scene, I thought of a mother laying down her own life to save her infant child's," Jon said. "Anne knew her own fate was inescapable but she had a chance for her death to count for something."

"You portrayed Anne Boleyn as a martyr?"

"Her motherly instincts overpowered her anger and resentment," he said. "She forgave her accuser and called him merciful. And she meant every word."

"How did that go over?" Emma asked.

"We never got the chance to perform it on account of the fire," Jon said. "Now the whole scene is missing."

"There are plenty of angry speeches throughout the play," Emma said. "So why was this one scene left out?"

"Will and I wanted to keep the scene because it was an historic fact," Jon said. "Some of us worried that defamation of the Tudor family could lead to unrest and resentment of the monarchy."

"You and William Shakespeare both wanted to keep the scene," Emma said. "Do you still have a copy of this original version?"

"No, it was lost. But I still remember every word."

"I believe you do," Emma said. "I don't believe you knew William Shakespeare."

"Will was my mentor," Jon said.

"Ryan told me you wept at Shakespeare's grave like he was a true friend," Emma said.

"I wonder what others stories he's told about me," Jon said. "Sometimes I say things that no one understands, like how I feel the past and present are blurred together."

"Have you had your head examined recently?"

"I was in the hospital a few weeks ago and they told me I was healthy when they released me," Jon said.

"Why were you in the hospital?" Emma asked.

"I don't really remember. Is it OK if I tell you later?"

"That's fine," Emma said. "I'm sorry if I'm asking so many personal questions. It's just that you have such a delightful imagination. Do you ever break out of character, like when you're alone?"

"What do you mean by that?" Jon asked.

A passenger train rumbled past on an elevated railway and Jon watched it with a mixture of fear and wonder.

"I mean that your act is very convincing, but do you ever stop pretending you're from the past and ignorant of modern technology?" she asked after the train passed.

"Yes," Jon said. "I'm not pretending to be from the past. I told you it blurs together. It's confusing. There are skyscrapers and smartphones now. I remember a different ending to *All is True* that was so surprising in its tenderness that everyone in the audience was brought to tears. It was sublime."

"Audiences were brought to tears by Anne Boleyn's farewell speech that was not included in the *First Folio* or in any other published version," Emma clarified. "I want to believe you, Jon. I really do."

They each purchased groceries for the week and carried them in cloth shopping bags. They were walking around the borough looking for a nice restaurant when Jon noticed an unusual smell.

"What is that?" he asked.

"That's curry," Emma said. "It's a spice they put on certain foods. Have you never tried Indian food?"

Jon said he hadn't so they got a table at the Indian restaurant. Jon didn't know what anything was. Emma ordered a sampler platter and a chicken curry entrée.

"Honesty is critical in any relationship," Jon said. He reached his hands halfway across the table and Emma met his hands with hers. "Without honesty you can't have trust, and without trust, real love is impossible. A lover can become your spouse and hold greater influence over your life than anyone else. Lovers should be chosen carefully and nurtured over time."

"I'm too trusting," Emma said. Her eyes were locked to his like their hands. "I was with someone once who was pathologically dishonest and I refused to see it, even when the signs were right in front of me."

"You should not do Anne's missing farewell speech until you are confident your performance will inspire reverence at her sacrifice, and not rage at its injustice," Jon said. "Your delivery must be perfect."

"I accept a worthy challenge," Emma said. "We should restage *All is True* with the original ending."

"I was thinking the same thing," Jon said.

Their food arrived and Jon was blown away by all the new flavors. Emma encouraged him to try different food combinations for a fuller experience.

"That was the most unusual and wonderful food experience I have ever had," he said as he placed a few notes on the bill to cover the tab plus tip. "Have you ever been to India?"

"No, and possibly neither has the cook," Emma said. "Have you ever had Chinese food?"

"From China? No, but now I want to try it."

"Maybe next time," Emma said. "I'm full of curry."

Jon walked Emma back to her apartment house with their groceries and stopped in front of her oak door. Emma looked into Jon's eyes and waited for him to say something.

"The first time I saw you, I thought I was dreaming," he said. "I never knew such a person as you could exist, and now I'm enamored of thee. You're my curry."

"Well, I can be pretty spicy at times," she said.

"Is two weeks long enough to know someone?" he asked. "We were already friends by our first Saturday, but I didn't want to rush. Then we started working together and we saw each other every day. Now I think about you all the time. I want to tell you how I feel, but I don't want things to get awkward at work."

"It won't get awkward," she said. "We'll keep it professional while we're at work, like how Carmen and Steve are together at rehearsals. The only drama will be the Shakespearean kind."

"I was a different person when we first met," Jon said. "I had nothing. You have changed my life and made everything possible. All my dreams are coming true and it's all because of you. You have been a good friend to me and I endeavor to be more than your friend and co-worker. Will thou be my girlfriend?"

Emma put her arms around Jon's neck and smiled.

"I thought you'd never ask," she said. "Yes!"

They moved closer, closed their eyes, and kissed for the first time.

Chapter Eleven

The next week, Emma received a package addressed to her at Shakespeare's Globe. She unwrapped it in front of her cast members as soon as it arrived.

Inside the box was a scarlet-colored Tudor dress made of satin and velvet that she recognized from a few weeks earlier. Also in the box was a handwritten message, two fifty-pound notes, a bodice, a farthingale underskirt, and her own pair of blood-red shoes.

Emma said she knew the sender but she didn't recognize the elegant handwriting on the note.

"Dearest Emma," she read from the note, "This dress once belonged to the Tudor family and was worn by queens and their ladies in waiting. Now that honor is yours. These shoes saved my life! Thank you again for everything. I hope you get all you deserve. Love, Anne."

"Someone named Anne gave you a £1,000 dress, shoes, and cash?" Carmen said. "That's some pretty nice fan mail."

"Should I be jealous?" Jon joked. He thought he was fortunate one of his neighbors was studying calligraphy.

"I met Anne just before I met you," Emma said. "We only spoke once but she made a lasting impression on me.

Perhaps it was the dress that made the impression."

"You should try it on," Jon suggested.

"I want to, but it looks too nice and too old," she said. "Her note said it once belonged to the Tudor family. Could it really be five hundred years old?"

"Did this Anne woman also look like she could have been five hundred years old?" Steve joked. "I'm pretty sure it's a reproduction."

"It looked fabulous on her," Emma said. She reached into the box.

"Look at that gold brocade," Carmen said as Emma removed the dress from the box and held it out. The fabric shimmered in the light.

"I've never seen a costume like this," Emma said. "It looks like it was made by elves or something. This embroidery is out of this world. It's more like a £5,000 dress. I don't think I can wear this."

"I think you have to," Jon said. Everyone looked at him. "If the five-hundred-year-old ghost of Anne Boleyn lent you her favorite dress – which is a work of art in itself – you are obliged to wear it in a performance."

"OK, you guys are right," Emma said. "It's probably not five hundred years old. But these fastenings are on the back and I will need some help getting into this thing."

"I can help," Jon and Carmen said simultaneously.

"Great," Emma said. "We'll be back."

Emma took the dress to her changing room and Jon and Carmen followed. The remaining actors looked to Larry for direction.

"There are plenty of scenes we can rehearse that don't

have the three main characters," Larry said.

Emma let Jon and Carmen inside the changing room and shut the door behind them. Emma set down the box with the dress and then took off her shoes and handed them to Carmen. Emma stepped closer to Jon and turned around to show him her back.

"Will you unzip my dress, sweetheart?" Emma asked.

Jon found the zipper and slowly pulled it downward. Emma's purple-and-white striped dress opened at the back to reveal her fair skin and a narrow, black bodice that only covered her bosom. Jon had never seen anything like it.

She slid the dress off her shoulders and it fell to her waist. Emma turned around, pulled the dress down to the floor, and stepped out of it. She was wearing matching black underwear and nothing else. Jon thought Emma was in great shape and was relieved he didn't see any tattoos or birthmarks.

"Wow, you've got a great body, Emma," Carmen said. "Doesn't Emma have a smoking hot body, Jon?"

"You look like you're getting excited," Emma said.

"It's the first time I've seen you without clothes on," Jon admitted. "Darling, you have a magnificent body. Thank you for the new mental image. My dreams just got a little spicier."

"You guys are dating and you haven't seen each other naked yet?" Carmen asked.

"I haven't seen anyone naked," Jon said.

"Could someone help me with this corset?" Emma asked. Carmen took it out of the box and loosened the fastenings so Emma could get inside. Emma put her arms through the side holes and pulled the bodice over her head.

When she had it on properly, Carmen helped her pull the fastening straps on the back.

"Tighter," Jon said. "You'll never get the dress to fit right unless the bodice straps are fully tightened."

"I can't get it any tighter," Carmen said.

"May I?" Jon asked. He got behind Emma and adjusted the straps. "Take a deep breath and hold it."

Emma drew in a deep breath and Jon quickly pulled the fastening straps an inch tighter to close the gap. He tied a knot in the back to keep the bodice secure.

"I can't breathe," Emma said.

"That's how you know it's on right," Jon said. He picked up the farthingale skirt and tied it around Emma's waist, which covered her long, bare legs. "Normally a lady would wear a petticoat beneath her bodice."

Carmen had the dress prepared and she and Jon helped Emma get her arms through the sleeves and pulled the dress over her head. They adjusted the dress at her waist and then smoothed it over the farthingale. Jon tightened the straps in the back so the satin front was smooth and shiny. Emma slipped on her shoes and her costume was complete.

The three actors left the changing room and returned to rehearsals with the rest of the cast members. All the men stood up when Emma entered the room.

"Wow," Steve said. "You look … older? I mean you look great, but like you're from a different time."

Carmen shot Steve a quizzical look but Steve did not seem to understand her body language.

"Thanks," Emma said. "It does not feel as great as it looks. I can barely breathe."

"It's perfect, my dear," Larry said. "Do you think you could wear it by next week? Maybe with alterations?"

"I would never alter this dress," she said.

"Perhaps other alterations?" Larry suggested.

"I could probably lose half a stone by next week," Emma said.

"Are you serious?" Carmen asked. "You don't have to lose weight. If it's too tight, just wear a different dress."

"I'll go on a diet for this dress," Emma said. "I don't mind. It's worth it. Just be warned: I can get a little moody when I don't get enough to eat."

"That's putting it mildly," Carmen said. "Just don't start smoking again."

"I need to get out of this dress before I pass out," Emma said. "Can you help me? All the ties are out of reach."

"Let me get a quick picture of you in the dress, first," Carmen said. She pulled out her smartphone, pointed it at Emma and tapped the screen. "Act like you're excited to wear the dress and not like you're being suffocated by it."

Carmen took a few more photos of Emma, then inspected the images. Emma and Jon returned to her private changing room. The door was shut when Carmen arrived and the handle was locked. She knocked twice.

"Guys? Need my help getting Emma undressed?"

"I think we can manage it, thanks," Jon answered.

Emma pressed her soft lips to his and wrapped her arms around his neck. Jon closed his eyes, reached his hands behind her back, and found the knot he had tied earlier. He pulled one string and the knot came undone. Jon imagined the dress laces were on his front instead of her back as he loosened them with Emma facing him.

Jon pulled himself free from her embrace but not their continuous eye contact. He lifted the skirt of her dress and pulled it up to her waist, revealing the white farthingale underneath. Jon bent forward and kissed Emma again and then broke off the kiss and gently pulled the dress up over her head. She raised her arms as the dress came off, and quickly resumed their embrace the moment it was off.

Jon untied and removed her farthingale, which exposed her long bare legs. His hands wandered to her thighs, and he could tell from her firm posterior that she was still wearing her heels. His hands moved up to untie the knot on the back of the corset as his lips moved his kisses to Emma's cheekbones, her earlobes, and down her neck to her collarbone. The unfastened corset expanded as Emma drew in a gasp of air.

Jon pulled the corset up over her head as Emma raised her arms. He put the corset in the dress box on top of the other clothes. Jon picked up Emma's purple-and-white dress and handed it to her, but Emma wasn't done kissing. She pulled him close for another passionate embrace, this time wearing only her black two-piece underwear. She slipped off his tweed jacket and began to unbutton his vest.

There was a loud knocking on the door.

"Are you sure you don't need any help?" Carmen asked. "You two are awful quiet in there."

"We're fine," Jon said. He held on to Emma's bare

shoulders and gently moved backward. He smiled and shook his head in disbelief. "Just give us a minute." He picked up Emma's purple-and-white dress and handed it to her again.

"You can take longer than a minute if you need to," Carmen said from the other side of the door.

Emma stepped into her dress, pulled it up to her waist, put her arms through, and reached behind her back to pull the zipper up. She got the zipper near the top between her shoulders, but she couldn't reach the rest of the way. She moved closer to Jon again. Instead of turning around to give him access to her zipper, she closed her eyes and pressed her lips to his once more. Jon's hands felt her back to locate the zipper and pulled it to the top.

"We're ready!" Emma said. "Oops! I still have the wrong shoes on."

She switched shoes and put all the costume clothes back in the dress box. Jon put his tweed jacket back on and opened the door. Carmen was waiting outside and her face was flushed red.

"I know what you were doing," Carmen said. "Can you save that for after work?"

"That's difficult when you're working twelve hours a day," Emma said.

"Tell me about it," Carmen said.

"Don't be jealous, my queen," Jon said. "This dress commands attention from all who see it, and likewise it demands many personal sacrifices from its host. It shines like a star in its own right, but it takes a star to wear a star."

"You think I'm a star?" Emma asked. Her eyes

sparkled as she gazed at Jon adoringly.

"You are scintillating, my love. Your true radiance shines from that dress with fervency."

"I wish my boyfriend talked to me that way," Carmen said to herself.

No one stood up when they returned to rehearsals.

"Still love the dress?" Larry asked.

"Now that I can finally breathe, I want to talk about my character," Emma said. "That dress gave me confidence to say a few things that have been bothering me for a while. Henry VIII was desperate for a son, and Anne Boleyn's uterus was the one thing Henry couldn't have. He confused lust for love, sacrificed his marriage, and risked his kingdom and empire for that young, sweet vessel that he hoped would give him a male heir. Henry didn't care about Catherine or Anne or any of his wives. He didn't want daughters because he despised women. At the end of this play, Henry proclaims he's a changed man upon Elizabeth's christening. Like Jon said, it's 'complete bollocks.' We don't even see Anne after act two, yet everyone talks about her uterus for the rest of the play. The sycophancy of this ending is nauseating."

"Well, it was a man's world," Larry said. "No one thought a queen could rule England without a king until Elizabeth I. Archbishop Cranmer prophesied her future in the final scene."

"Henry had Anne beheaded when Elizabeth was three years old, and he married Jane Seymour less than two weeks later," Emma said. "That's not in the play, nor is there mention of Henry's other three wives. I wonder why

Shakespeare left that out. He didn't flatter tyrants in his other histories."

"I think Jon's ending was much better," Carmen said.

"Definitely," Steve said. "This play was originally called *All is True*. They probably changed the name after they changed the ending."

"How do you know the original ending, Jon?" Larry asked. "Or what you claim to be the original version."

"The play was the same but for the final two scenes," Jon said. "In the version I remember, Anne was put on trial in scene four and executed. Scene five took place nine years later. A very fat King Henry boasted about all his accomplishments to his son Edward. He said God chose him to rule England, just as God chose Edward to be the next sovereign ruler. And he warned his son about the high price of greatness."

"You were in this play?" Larry clarified. "In 1613?"

"Like Steve says, it was called *All is True*," Jon said.

"And you are the only person alive who remembers the true ending?" Larry asked.

"Evidently," Jon said. "No, I don't have proof."

"How did you stage Anne's actual execution?" Larry asked. "You have piqued my curiosity."

"The first two nights I read Anne's last words on my knees," Jon said. "Everyone was brought to tears. When I finished, the executioner approached the prisoner's dock with a broadsword and stood over Anne. The headsman raised his sword so the whole theater could see and brought it down swiftly. Ben stopped before actually striking me and gave my neck a gentle touch, which signaled me to collapse to the floor."

"That sounds frighteningly barbaric," Larry said.

"People were enraged, and we decided to skip the execution part itself for the third show," Jon said. "Ben wanted to use the trap door but he was overruled."

"Ben Jonson, the playwright?" Emma asked.

"That's right," Jon said. "Did he become famous?"

"I have an idea for the execution that could satisfy all these ghosts," Larry said. "Jon, will you write down the last two scenes of act five to the best of your recollection?"

"I'm an actor, not a writer," Jon said.

"I realize that, Jon, but could you write down what you remember?" Larry asked. "I need to know everything you know."

"Verily, I don't write," Jon said. "But I can dictate it to someone."

"I can help Jon write down the last two scenes," Emma volunteered.

"Thank you, Emma, and thank you, Jon," Larry said. "Don't forget the four of you have a photo shoot on Saturday evening in Hyde Park."

"What are we shooting?" Jon asked.

"We are shooting promotional photographs for our play, which opens next Wednesday," Larry said. "Do you know how to ride a horse?"

"Who doesn't?" Jon answered.

"Excellent," Larry said. "Let's meet at the Globe at five o'clock on Saturday evening. We will get into costume here and then travel to the park by motor carriage, where the horses will await."

* * *

Larry made an announcement to the cast during Wednesday's rehearsal.

"I shared our ideas for an alternate ending with our producers and higher-ups," Larry said. "They loved it and want to perform the play with the historically accurate, alternate ending and rename the production to *All is True*. We will use the script Jon dictated, and he shall have co-authorship with Shakespeare and Fletcher."

* * *

Jon went to watch his friends perform in the final showing of *Twelfth Night* on Friday evening. He sat in the center gallery opposite the stage on the second level, which he considered the best seat in the house apart from the floor directly in front of the stage.

He thought Emma's final portrayal of the manservant Cesario was more believable, more realistic, and funnier than the performance he saw three weeks earlier.

Jon waited in the box office with the other fans after the performance to greet the actors. As soon as he saw her, Jon gave Emma a bouquet with a dozen crimson roses.

"Outstanding performance tonight, my love," Jon said. "I thoroughly enjoyed your duality."

Emma gave Jon a tight hug and a kiss on the lips.

"I've been burning my candle at both ends and there's almost nothing left," Emma said. "I want to give you my undivided attention, but my brain is crammed full of two different Shakespeare plays, I haven't slept for weeks, I'm always hungry, and I just want to go home, open a bottle of wine, and let my poor brain relax."

"You should," Jon said.

"I've quit drinking," Emma said. "I can't afford the calories and I'm a total lightweight when I'm dieting. I'm just going to fall asleep as soon as I get home."

"I'll walk you home," Jon said. "Let's plan for a nice supper somewhere tomorrow, after the photo shooting on horseback."

"We could make it a double date," Emma suggested. "Do you mind if I invite Carmen and Steve? We can bail on them if it gets dull."

Carmen and Steve were both in the box office.

"It's fine with me," Jon said.

"Do you guys want to join us for supper tomorrow after the photo shoot?" Emma asked Carmen and Steve.

"Sure," Carmen said. "Do you have a reservation?"

"No, Jon just thought of it," Emma said. She took out her smartphone. "Somewhere close, with a killer view."

"I'll help look," Carmen said as she took out her own smartphone and began tapping on it. "I got us a table for four at the Tate Modern's restaurant on the ninth floor of the switch house. Perks of being a member."

"Thanks, Carmen," Jon said. "See you again in the morrow. Bye, Steve."

"Take care, you guys," Steve said.

Jon held hands with Emma as they walked to her apartment house. They hugged in front of her door and kissed goodnight.

* * *

The next afternoon, Jon met Emma, Steve, Carmen, and Larry at the Globe, and the actors changed into their characters' costumes for the first time.

Jon put on a pair of long white stockings that showed off his legs and slipped on a pair of white leather shoes. He put on a wide sixteenth-century doublet with fake silver brocade, white breeches, and then a white jerkin with extra-wide shoulders and puffy sleeves. Jon placed fake furs over his wide shoulders, added several sparkling costume necklaces and rings, and topped it with a fur cap.

Jon used spirit gum to affix a bushy, reddish-brown beard to his chin, which he then stylized based on a portrait of Henry VIII that was taped to his makeup mirror. Jon attached the largest codpiece he could find in the prop area to his midsection.

"I love it!" Larry said when he saw the four actors in costume.

Emma was wearing a blue Renaissance dress and wore her hair braided over a headpiece. She wore leather riding boots with matching leather gloves.

Carmen wore a conservative, black dress with white accents and a white hat that completely covered her hair. She wore several golden costume necklaces.

Steve was also dressed conservatively in black pants and a white bishop's smock. He had a bishop's collar and a large ring on the smallest finger of his left hand.

"Remember," Larry said as he walked the four actors to the van parked outside, "we are taking promotional photos for the play. Your job is to act like your character for the photos. Do whatever Atlas says. I'm leaving but this van will stay here to take you back to the Globe. I will see you on Monday. Have fun!"

Everyone put on their seat belts. The van started and the driver took them past Westminster Abbey, Parliament, and Buckingham Palace before delivering them at the southeast corner of Hyde Park.

Jon saw the four hackneys awaiting them in leather saddles. He noticed their saddles had horns in front.

"Are we doing everything on horseback?" Jon asked Atlas, the photographer.

"There are a few places we can dismount for a photo, but mostly I want to get the four of you together in a single frame, on horseback," Atlas said. "Why do you ask?"

"I was wondering if I should leave my codpiece in the van," Jon said. He thought Atlas sounded effeminate.

Atlas had a young and beardless face, and silver hair that was kept short in the back, and wore cargo pants, a vest, and backpack loaded with photography equipment.

"Oh, you will definitely want to keep it on for historical accuracy," Emma said. "Henry filled that codpiece with his enormous ego."

"I think you should wear it," Atlas said.

Jon got out of the van and adjusted his costume, then studied the horses from a distance. He remembered his previous encounter with a horse that had nearly killed him and hesitated his approach. He told himself he had no reason to be afraid. That animal had been spooked and was improperly restrained. Jon and Will were in its path. These were different horses. Jon knew it wasn't fair to blame all horses for the actions of one.

Jon had been riding horses for half his life, and they were the only available mode of transportation aside from walking. His experience reassured him and he approached the horses with renewed confidence.

"What fine, noble creatures," Jon said in character. He knew Henry VIII was an expert horseman. "Which one is worthy enough to carry a monarch?"

"You shall ride Pegasus," Atlas said and led Jon to the tallest and proudest stallion. The animal was brown like nutmeg, with a white diamond between its eyes and white stockings on all four legs.

Jon looked the great animal in one eye, let it smell his hand and gently stroked its long nose.

"Le cheval volant," Jon said to the horse in a soothing voice. "Is it true? Can you fly us into the clouds?"

"Go ahead and mount your horses and then we will proceed to the first location," Atlas said.

Emma was able to mount her horse without assistance. Steve helped Carmen onto her horse and then struggled to keep his horse still while he mounted. Eventually he succeeded.

Pegasus stood perfectly still as Jon put his foot in one stirrup. He grabbed the saddle horn with one hand and leapt into the saddle. He put his other foot in the stirrup and adjusted his codpiece. Jon felt like a king on top of the horse. He grabbed the reins and spoke to the horse again.

"Pegasus, fly!" he shouted and kicked its sides with his heels. The horse shot forward at a full gallop into the park. They reached a clearing after traveling about half a kilometer through dense forest. Jon slowed Pegasus to a canter and then to a trot as they waited for the others to catch up. He looked back and didn't see his friends, Atlas, or anyone whatsoever, so he turned Pegasus around and they trotted back toward the entrance.

"Thou art a prince of palfreys," Jon said to his horse, playfully paraphrasing a scene from *Henry V*. "I feel like Perseus bounding from the earth and soaring through the air like a hawk. Thou art made of pure air and fire. Henceforth, all other jades I shall call beasts."

Pegasus was interested in an area to the west of the entrance which made Jon curious as well. This was Jon's first time inside the 350-acre park that became Henry VIII's hunting grounds after he seized the land from the monks of Westminster Abbey in 1536.

Jon and Pegasus explored the winding paths of the rose garden for several minutes. He could not recall another garden that smelled even half as heavenly. His horse kept reaching for a particularly plump blossom.

"Pegasus," Jon said to the horse. "What's in a name? That which we call a rose by any other name would smell as sweet."

Jon heard a faint clicking noise unlike any bird he could identify. He looked for its source and he spotted Atlas taking pictures of him from a short distance. Jon imagined he really was Henry VIII and would do as he pleased in Hyde Park.

"It's OK, Pegasus," he said. "Sweeten thine breath with a few of my royal roses."

Pegasus eagerly devoured the delicate rose petals. The gardeners would not be amused but Jon thought it was harmless and hilarious. He belted out a hearty laugh and the clicking noise returned.

Jon stroked the horse's mane and saw Atlas looking at the back of the camera and smiling.

"Come now, that's enough," Jon said to the horse. "We must return."

They trotted over to the photographer.

"That was inspired, your excellency. Next, I wish to take some pictures of all four characters together."

Jon reached down, picked a rose, and smelled it. He thought of Emma and signaled to Pegasus to take them in search of the others. He rode at a canter until he spotted and rejoined his party. Jon approached Emma – who was also on horseback – and handed her the rose, which she accepted. Carmen watched them with envy.

Atlas rode up to the group pedaling a metal frame that was attached to two wheels, one in front of the other.

"Let's head into the meadow next, but I want to go ahead to get your approach," Atlas said. "I will signal you when I'm ready."

Atlas pedaled to the meadow as the four riders waited for the signal.

"I think we should trot four abreast," Jon said. "When we get about halfway, I propose we should race to the finish. It will look sporty."

"Sounds fun," Steve said. "You might not win."

Atlas made it to the meadow and waved at the group.

"That's the signal," Jon said, and he proceeded forward. The other three riders joined alongside at a trot.

Their trotting gate was a little too slow and bumpy for the riders, so Jon sped up to a canter and the other three horses adjusted their speeds to stay aligned. Jon found if he stood up in his saddle, his codpiece wouldn't jostle his bollocks as much.

When the horses approached the midpoint of their journey, Carmen's horse shot forward at a full gallop. Her example was quickly followed by Emma and Steve. Jon now found himself in the back of the group.

"Make like the wind, Pegasus," Jon said and gave his horse another small kick in the sides.

Pegasus appeared to understand and flew into a racing gallop. Jon quickly overtook Steve, then Emma, and soon he was racing alongside Carmen.

She looked at Jon with an intensity he assumed was a competitive spirit and he flashed her a joyous smile. Her expression changed and Carmen smiled back.

Pegasus reached the area next to the photographer's mountain bike first, and both horses slowed to a halt.

Carmen was still smiling when Emma and Steve caught up with them. Jon smiled at Emma and they both laughed as they caught their breath. Everyone was happy, and Atlas seemed especially so.

"These are some of the best promotional photographs I have ever taken," Atlas said and then addressed Jon specifically. "You are one of the most photogenic models I have ever encountered. You have raw talent. Have you done any professional modeling?"

"This was my first attempt modeling on horseback for promotional photographs," Jon said.

"You're a natural," Atlas said and handed Jon a card. "These shots are pure gold. Call me."

"I think she likes you," Emma said after Atlas left.

"She?" Jon asked. "I thought he was an old man."

They rode back to the gate, dismounted, and climbed into the same van they rode in earlier. The driver returned them safely to the Globe.

The four actors removed their makeup, got out of their costumes, and changed back into their own clothes. They were just in time for their reservation and they crossed the street to the Tate Modern, a former industrial power plant that was retrofitted to house a world-class collection of modern art. The museum was closed for the day but there were at least fifty people waiting for a table at the restaurant.

Carmen walked to the front of the queue and showed the doorman her photo identification and museum membership card. He checked his list and let the four of them inside immediately.

They walked through the lobby to a bank of metal doors. Carmen pressed a button on the wall and it lit up.

"What's this?" Jon asked.

"The restaurant is on the ninth floor," Carmen said.

A bell rang and the metal doors in front of them slid open to reveal a smaller room. Carmen, Emma, and Steve went inside and waited for Jon to follow. He stepped into the room and the metal doors slid shut.

Jon felt the floor jolt upward and adjusted his footing to compensate. He looked at the other occupants and everyone seemed relaxed and unconcerned.

"I love your dress, Carmen," Emma said.

Carmen was wearing a sleeveless, crimson dress with matching shoes and lip gloss.

"Thanks," Carmen said. "It's not a museum artifact but it can still catch a man's eye."

Emma was wearing a black cocktail dress that Jon thought looked both elegant and semiformal.

There was another bell sound, the movement stopped, and the metal doors slid open to reveal an entirely different room. Carmen and Emma exited the lift and Jon waited next to Steve.

"After you," Steve said. He extended an arm out the doorway.

Jon stepped into the room and Steve followed. The restaurant had dim lighting that focused on the tables and made it easier to observe the stunning view of London from the large glass windows that wrapped around the outer walls.

The maître d' greeted them and showed them to their table next to a window overlooking the river Thames, St. Paul's, and the great city beyond. Jon had never been this high up before. He leaned his head onto the glass window and looked straight down. He could see Shakespeare's Globe below, but its interior lights were turned off.

The waiter arrived and took their orders.

"Hey, do you guys remember that Renaissance fair in Stratford?" Carmen asked. They all said they did. "I remember Jon sang 'Greensleeves' to me during our first dance together."

"And you loved it," Jon said. Carmen smiled.

"I remember the next dance better," Steve said.

"Oh, that's right!" Carmen said. "You were dancing with that hussy and I rescued you by cutting in."

"Clearly, I needed rescuing," Steve said. "That hussy started dancing with Jon without missing a beat."

"I was just being a gentleman," Jon said. "Or I was aspiring to be one, which is just as good. She wasn't my type. She was way too young, silly, and plain for me."

Jon gently squeezed Emma's hand and she smiled.

"Where were you again?" Carmen asked Emma. "You ghosted us the whole day and then made up a story about meeting some guy."

"I was being stupid," Emma said. "I should've found you guys. I felt like a ghost visiting those old places."

"I know what you mean," Jon said. "These ghosts appear when you least expect them. I just realized both Catherine and Anne were dead and Henry was on his third wife when he seized Hyde Park in 1536. The scenes we photographed today never happened."

Their meal arrived on large white plates that were speckled with colorful sauces.

Jon had a grilled lamb shank over cooked corn and black beans. Steve's meal was a medium-rare steak that arrived pre-cut and on top of a bed of steamed broccoli. Carmen had grilled cauliflower with caper-raisin dressing and cashew butter. Emma ordered a salad and all the vegetables arrived cut into long ribbons.

"I liked your Henry VIII beard today," Carmen said. "It looks masculine and appropriate for your role."

"Thank you," Jon said. "I'm glad you like it. I have a friend who wears false beards who showed me his secret."

Emma looked at Jon with astonishment.

"I'm only kidding!" Jon laughed. "Have you guys

met Emma's brother Ryan?"

"I didn't know you had a brother," Carmen said.

"He's handsome, and a bachelor, too," Jon said. "Like Emma, but with a beard. I'll introduce you sometime. Ryan is old-fashioned like me."

"There's nobody like you, Jon," Emma said.

"You think who is handsome?" Steve asked. He finished his meal and set down his fork. "I have a real beard. You don't like it anymore? I can shave it off."

"It's your face," Carmen said. "Do what you want."

"Maybe I will," Steve said. "You should have the biggest beard on stage, King Henry. You deserve it."

"Why do you always do that?" Carmen asked.

"What do I always do?" Steve asked.

"You submit to Jon like he's your captain," she said.

"What's wrong with that?" Steve asked. "I respect Jon, and want to be more like him."

"Am I an obstacle to your infatuation?" she asked. "Emma and I can leave you two together if you need some male bonding time."

"You're the one who's infatuated," Steve said, then he changed his voice to a higher tone to mimic Carmen. "'I love your fake beard, Jon. It's so masculine!'"

"I know I'm crushing on you," Emma said and she locked eyes with Jon. They squeezed each other's hands tenderly.

The waiter asked if they needed anything else and then handed Jon the bill. Jon pulled out a wad of cash.

"Allow me to get the bill tonight," Jon said. "You guys have been so kind and generous to me these past few weeks. It's the least I can do. I had a great time today, and I want to thank you guys for everything."

Everyone smiled as Jon counted out a pile of bills. He was cashless after paying the bill and tip, but would have enough money to buy a new suit after his next payday.

"Thanks for supper, Jon," Emma said. She leaned over to him, closed her eyes, and kissed him on the lips. "It's too stuffy in here. Let's get some air."

"We shall be birds of prey," Jon said. Emma took Jon's hand and pulled him down the hallway to the lift. "We'll catch up with you guys on Monday," Jon said to Steve and Carmen on his way out of the restaurant.

"Thanks, Jon," Steve said. "Have a great weekend!"

"You two be safe tonight," Carmen said.

The lift doors opened from the center and Jon and Emma went inside. Emma pressed the button for the ground floor and the doors closed.

Jon and Emma were alone together for the first time in days. They quickly pressed their bodies together and kissed just as the floor dropped an inch and began its descent. Jon felt his heart jump in Emma's warm embrace. He wanted to hold her and kiss her forever.

The doors slid open at the ground floor, and half a dozen people stood outside the lift waiting to go in. Jon and Emma laughed when they noticed they were being watched, and they exited the lift so the others could ride up to the restaurant.

Jon and Emma walked arm-in-arm down the well-lit streets to Jon's apartment building.

"Would you like to come up?" he asked. "I'm on top."

Emma answered with another long kiss and then they climbed the four flights of stairs together.

"It's not a mess, but I need to tidy up just a bit," Jon said when they reached his door on the fourth floor. "Do you mind waiting out here for just a minute?"

Jon went inside his apartment and shut the door. He reemerged a few minutes later, offered his hand to Emma, guided her inside, and closed the door behind her.

Jon's apartment was dark except for the city lights shining through the large windows and from about three dozen lit candles arranged in clusters around the room.

"Do you like the candles?" he asked. "I think they help to unveil the bright lights outside. I prefer my view of the city to the restaurant's."

"I also prefer this view and I wish to unveil it further," she said.

Emma slipped her hands inside Jon's jacket and slid them up his chest to his shoulders. She pulled him forward and their lips met for a hungry kiss. She slipped his jacket off and it dropped to the floor.

Jon's hands massaged her back until they found the zipper on the back of her black dress. She began to unknot and remove his necktie as Jon slid her zipper down her back. He removed his vest and unbuttoned his shirt while she slid out of her dress.

"Do you always wear a girdle?" she asked after Jon removed his shirt. Emma was wearing a silk chemise the color of lavender. She was not wearing a bodice.

"Not always," Jon said as he untied and removed his girdle. "See? I'm not wearing one now."

He still had on an undershirt that tied at the collar and around his wrists. He unbuckled and removed his trousers, stepped out of his shoes and unbuckled the garter belts holding up his black stockings.

"How many layers are you wearing?" she asked.

Emma pulled Jon's second shirt off over his head and tossed it to the floor. She pressed her hands on his bare chest, then raised her arms as Jon pulled her lavender chemise off over her head and tossed it to the floor.

He pulled Emma in for another long kiss. Jon still wore breeches but his stockings had dropped to the floor. Emma's black push-up brassiere and matching underpants were the next articles to go, followed by Jon's breeches.

Jon and Emma stood before each other for the first time without costumes or disguises. In the candlelight, Jon imagined Emma was a statue carved from a single block of marble. The embodiment of feminine beauty pressed herself against him and Jon felt himself harden into stone.

"Do you think we should …?" he asked between the kisses he planted like seeds of love on her earlobes, the nape of her neck, her collarbone and shoulders, and softly down her arms to her hands.

"Definitely," she said as she returned his kisses in the same fashion. "Do you have one?"

"Have what?" he asked.

"A contraceptive," Emma said. "It's a must for dating in the twenty-first century."

"We could wait," he said, and dropped to one knee.

Emma made a tiny gasp. Jon softly kissed her chest and ribcage. She let out another sigh and slowly ran her fingers through his soft hair.

"We could wait, but we don't have to be married first," she said. "This isn't the sixteenth century and I'm not Anne Boleyn. I want you, Jon Henry. But you need to know something about me first. I was married once and it didn't work out. Now I'm divorced and I'm free to be with whomever I choose. I choose you. But I'm in no rush to remarry. Let's take it sl… Ooh! A little lower, please."

Jon kissed her hips, thighs, and kneecaps. He moved his kisses up her sides to her bosom, then up her neck until their mouths met again.

"Should we wait or continue?" he asked. His fingers gently caressed and pinched her sensitive places.

"Please continue," she said. "The mood is perfect."

"First, you should know something about me."

"What is it?" Emma asked.

"I have not done this for a very long time," he said. "It feels like it has been centuries."

"Experience is the greatest tutor," she said. "Don't worry about impressing me the first time. Do you have a contraceptive?"

"No, I don't think so."

"I brought my favorite kind, so we're both in luck," Emma said, and took a plastic wrapper out of her purse.

They moved over to Jon's mattress and got more comfortable. Jon laid on his back with his hands behind his head.

Emma began kissing Jon's chin and neck and covered his chest with dozens of kisses before moving lower. He closed his eyes and felt her soft hair stroke his body. Her

kisses strengthened his desire. Jon imagined rolling on a silk stocking that covered his entire leg.

Emma climbed on top of Jon and looked him in the eyes. He felt so safe and confident in her loving gaze that Jon wished he could dive into the clear pools of her eyes and swim in their warm waters.

"I love thee more than I love mine own life," he said. "Before I met you, I was lost at sea in a hopeless tempest. You are the beacon that saved this lost sailor and you are the rock upon which I have built my whole life. I am at home with you."

"I love my life when I'm with you," Emma said. "You are my rock as I am yours. Let's build our first castle tonight. Welcome home."

Two became one and created a bridge between souls born four hundred years apart. Centuries were slowly rubbed away as the past and the future united together to become the eternal present.

Jon imagined he was a stallion with its mare or a cock pairing with its hen. It was the oldest dance in the world, yet there were new moves and techniques to master. The dancers alternated positions and took turns leading.

When they tired of the bed, the lovers moved to the couch and their athletic bodies continued exploring the possibilities of their coupling. Jon felt his passion for Emma grow deeper with every minute.

Eventually, their love became too steamy for the leather couch and they rolled on to the hardwood floor. They tried a few positions on the countertop, the table and chairs, and every other place they could think of in Jon's apartment before they returned to his mattress.

The smaller candles went out long before the lovers had finished, leaving only the largest candles still burning. The dimmer glow made his apartment feel more intimate.

Jon laid on his back and stared at the ceiling while Emma rested her head on his right shoulder. His right arm was cuddled between her right arm and her bosom. They both had satisfied expressions on their faces.

"Some have greatness thrust upon them," Emma said. Her eyes were closed. "Tell me about your childhood."

"My father was a mercer, as was his father before him. I attended grammar school with my older brothers and sisters. We used to fish and play in the river Avon."

"Ryan told me your house burned down," she said. "When did that happen?"

"While we were at school," Jon said. "We came home one day and everything was gone. My father told us we were moving to my uncle's and there was nothing to pack. He looked defeated, like his spirit was broken. I don't recall my mother smiling again."

"I'm sorry," she said. "That's a sad story. Where did you move to after the fire?"

"Our family split apart," he said. "My parents and youngest siblings moved in with my uncle in Shottery. My two oldest brothers became apprentices with other mercers, and my two older sisters married men from London. I never found out what happened to them. I was sent to boarding school. There were definitely some sad times, but I try to focus on the happier moments. What about yourself? What's your story?"

"Normal childhood, went to university," she said. "My parents still live in the same house I grew up in, and whenever I go home it feels like traveling back in time."

"You mentioned you were married before," he said. "Do you still see your ex-husband?"

"He's also an actor," she said. "Occasionally our paths converge socially. He's handsome, charismatic, and persuasive, but I know him to be a pathological liar. His only truth is what he desires to be true."

"Lies spoil the mind like a rotten apple spoils the barrel," Jon said. "My mother told me to always tell the truth because you won't have to remember anything. Your ex could be very confused about his true self."

"Do you still talk to your mother?" Emma asked.

"I speak to her in my prayers," he said. "She died when she was our age."

Jon closed his eyes and pictured his mother's face. Her spirit was smiling in his mind. He cried softly at his bittersweet memories.

"How did she die?" Emma asked. Her own eyes were filled with tears.

"She died of the plague," he said. "The Black Death took her sweet soul to heaven with everyone else."

Emma wiped her eyes and she frowned.

"Did you just say the plague?" she asked.

"Thirty-thousand people died from it in 1603," Jon said. "My family was still living in my uncle's house in Shottery, and they were all quarantined together. I didn't get to see them to say goodbye, and none of us could write. Is there now a cure for the plague?"

"Yes, there's a cure. You just said your family died from the plague in 1603. How did they really die?"

"What do you mean?" he asked. He wiped his eyes.

"You can't expect me to believe your family died of the plague," she said. "Why are you telling me this? Tell me the truth, Jon. Was it cancer, influenza, a virus?"

"They died in scorching pain, vomiting and defecating blood," he said as tears ran down his face. "I wish I knew why bad things happen to good people. My mother deserved a better death than that, but we don't always get what we deserve. Death takes everyone, and some he takes sooner than others."

"Damn you, Jon!" Emma said and she stood up. "I can't believe you! You're making me crazy! How can you be such an amazing lover with such a deep character flaw that compels you to lie about your own mother for the sake of a fantasy? You need to be real with me right now!"

Jon sat up in bed. Emma had changed from tender to hostile like an unexpected thunderstorm.

"I swear as a gentleman, on my mother's grave, I am telling you the truth," he pledged.

"That was the wrong answer," Emma said, and she began to get dressed in the dark. "I feel like such an idiot. I keep making the same mistake and falling for actors. A real gentleman would not lie to his lover about his own mother unless he had a mental illness. I love a fantasy as much as the next person, but I also need to stop at some point and be my real self. Your fantasy never stops, but this is where I get off."

Emma was fully dressed and ready to leave.

"I think you're wearing my clothes," he said.

Emma clicked the light switch next to the door but the room remained dark. She clicked the switch on and off.

"Why are your lights out?" she asked.

"They asked if I needed electricity. I said I didn't."

There was light coming under the door from the hallway so Emma opened the door wide enough to confirm she was indeed dressed in Jon's blue tweed suit, and she was also wearing his leather shoes. She shut the door, put her hands on her head, and cursed in frustration.

"What the hell am I doing?" she yelled to herself, then deliberately calmed her tone. "Can I please borrow this?"

"That's my only outfit," he said.

Emma carefully removed the tweed jacket, vest, and pants and unbuttoned the shirt with her back to Jon. She took off the shirt and began looking for her black dress in the dark wearing only her black undergarments. Emma stole a quick glance at Jon. He was up and lighting a few more candles.

"Will you help me find my dress?" she asked.

Jon brought his tall candle over and they found her garments in a corner. She put on her silk chemise and stepped into her black dress and then her shoes. She turned her back to Jon, and he zipped her dress closed.

Emma turned around and looked into Jon's eyes. She seemed confused and insecure.

"I want you to stay," he said with confidence.

She looked down and was surprised to see his intentions were corroborated by more than words.

"I freaked out, and I'm sorry you had to see that," she

said. "I'm sorry I tried to psychoanalyze you. I think I'm still in love with you, but right now I should go home."

"We have a big week ahead," he said. "We don't need to rush things. I can walk you home if you want. You're welcome to join me for church tomorrow morning. I also understand if you need a little break from my fantasy."

"I spent every waking hour with you for three weeks and I still haven't figured you out," she said. "I need some time off to recharge. I will see you at work on Monday."

Emma gave Jon a friendly parting hug.

"This was the best night of my life," Jon said. He felt his heart melt as he looked into her watery eyes with wonder. He closed his eyes and they kissed again.

Chapter Twelve

Every seat in Shakespeare's Globe was filled and the floor area was packed with groundlings. Every face was focused on the action taking place on stage.

King Henry VIII had just pardoned Archbishop Cranmer and asked him to baptize the princess Elizabeth at the end of act five, scene three. Jon, Steve, and the other actors went backstage and two actors playing the porters came on shouting insults at the groundlings.

"Belong to the gallows, and be hanged, ye rude slaves!" the porter yelled. "Leave your gaping! Do not look for ale and cakes here, ye rogues!"

The porter's man held the porter back from striking an audience member.

"Pray, sir, be patient," the porter's man said. "Tis as much impossible, unless we sweep them from the door with cannons!"

"How got they in, and be hanged?" the porter asked.

"Alas, I know not," the porter's man answered. "How gets the tide in?"

The porter walked to the front of the stage along a raised walkway to a small section of stage that extended into the center of the theater. He began setting up four posts connected with rope to outline the dock.

The porter's man followed him out onto the stage.

"What hast thou heard?" he asked.

"I heard the king had a nasty fall whilst jousting," the porter confided. "King Henry was asleep for two hours, almost as long as some people here."

There was laughter in the audience but the actors kept going without a pause.

"The king survived," the porter's man said.

"He did, but he was never the same," the porter answered. "His mind changed about so many things."

"Like the queen?"

"Aye," the porter answered. "When the queen learned the news of his fall, she fell herself, and a few days later, she lost their unborn baby boy."

"A prince?" the porter's man asked. "How tragic!"

"For her," the porter said. "I heard it was her third miscarriage. That's what this trial is all about."

"I heard she had an affair with her brother, and he was the father of the unborn child," the porter's man said.

"Slander!" the porter said. "Don't believe a word of it. Today we'll hear the disgraced queen try to explain her actions and offer clarity. His grace could pardon her majesty but it's unlikely."

The porter and his man left the posts and rope outlining the dock and they went backstage. Jon came out dressed as King Henry VIII wearing the same beard and costume he wore for the photo shoot in Hyde Park the previous Saturday.

Henry sat on his throne at the back of the stage, facing

the audience and the dock. Another woman sat to Henry's left, in the seat last occupied by Anne Boleyn.

"Enter the accused to stand trial," Henry said.

Emma came on stage for the first time since act two and a few audience members cried out at her changed appearance. No longer dressed as a Tudor queen, she wore a soiled nightgown without a bodice, farthingale, or dress. Her hair was messy, her bare hands and feet were dirty, and her skin looked thin and unhealthy. Anne's execution had been postponed twice before, and she had already accepted her own fate as inevitable.

Emma walked to end of the dock in the center of the theater and turned to face the throne. Steve stood to Jon's right, dressed as Archbishop Cranmer.

"Anne Boleyn, you have been charged with high treason, incest, adultery, and witchcraft," Cranmer said. "This court has found you guilty of all charges, and your sentence is death by beheading. If you have any last words, you may speak them now."

"I am come hither to accuse no man," Anne began, "nor to speak anything of that, whereof I am accused and condemned to die, but I pray God save the king and send him long to reign over you, for a gentler nor a more merciful prince was there never: and to me he was ever a good, a gentle and sovereign lord."

A tear ran down her face as she made her final plea.

"If any person will meddle of my cause, I require them to judge the best," she continued. "And thus, I take my leave of the world and of you all, and I heartily desire you all to pray for me."

The executioner's broadsword glimmered as it was slowly unsheathed.

"O Lord have mercy on me, to God I commend my soul!" Emma cried out to the whole theater.

Jon and the other actors on stage froze and the orchestra began playing a macabre melody.

There was movement in the groundling area and hundreds of heads turned to see what was happening. The actor who portrayed the late Duke of Buckingham walked through the audience and climbed up a small set of stairs by the dock. He wore the same soiled clothing for his own trial at the start of act two, and his face was painted white.

Buckingham's ghost looked at Anne but said not a word as he slowly circled the four posts that made the dock. He was followed on stage by the actor who portrayed Cardinal Wolsey. The disgraced cardinal was wearing scarlet pajamas, and his face was also painted white. He stared at Anne but said nothing as he followed the duke around the dock.

A third ghost climbed out of the audience onto the stage. Catherine of Aragon wore a white silk gown and a crown made of thorns. Carmen's face was also painted white like the others.

Anne was most frightened by the ghost of Catherine but all three spirits moved in a steady, slow circle. They had been enemies in life, but held no animosity in death. Anne reached out her hand and the ghosts stopped moving.

Catherine looked Anne in the eyes and slowly lifted the crown of thorns off her own head and placed it onto Anne's head. Catherine and Anne held hands.

The four ghosts circled the dock once more before descending the small stairs. They moved in single file through the stunned audience and out the main exit.

As soon as the ghosts departed, the attention turned to King Henry. Jon felt the audience throwing silent knives and daggers with their angry eyes as the scene changed around him, but he remained motionless and stone-faced.

The dock disappeared, and two stage hands carried out a large chest plate that had fur-covered shoulders and a massive pot belly. They set the prop over Jon's torso as he sat on his throne, which made him appear to double in size. His crown was replaced with a larger crown. Someone put a gilded scepter in his left hand and a large smoked turkey leg in his right hand.

The actress portraying Henry's third wife stood up and walked off stage, and a different actress portraying Henry's sixth wife gracefully took the seat to Henry's left.

An eight-year-old boy came on stage wearing fur slippers and play clothes made of shiny silk. The boy was occupied with a small, wooden toy.

Jon bit into the turkey leg and tore off a bite, then he began to yell with a mouthful of meat.

"God willing, you shall rule this kingdom for fifty years, my young Prince Edward," Henry shouted, and bits of meat fell out of his mouth as he spoke. "You must be a wise and a just king like me. I am the greatest monarch this world will ever know. Time shall never erase my name! I created a new religion, built up Parliament and amassed a navy to rival France and Spain. Mine enemies tremble at the very thought of me. I believe God almighty chose me for this divine mission."

The boy played with his toy and listened to his father. The toy broke, and the boy began to cry. Henry took another bite of his turkey leg.

"You there!" Henry yelled at a minion. "Thy royal prince needs a different toy!"

The servant scurried off stage, and the boy stopped crying. He looked at his father and wiped away his tears.

"Thou shalt be the next king," Henry said to his son. "You must crush your enemies before they crush you, as I crushed Scotland. Trust no one. Suspect everything. Even your own servants could be plotting against you."

The servant came out with a new curiosity that was brighter and shinier than the first. Edward smiled and clapped his hands.

"The prince does not play with broken toys," Henry said. He coughed and spat on the ground. "You shall invite the royal toymaker to make his home in our Tower until he can explain what happened to the prince's plaything."

"Off with his head!" the prince yelled.

Henry shook his head to nullify the prince's order.

"Son, you can't kill everyone, or there will be no one left to rule," Henry said. "You don't understand the power of your actions yet, but know that if you can learn to listen to the truth in your heart, you will always be right. You were chosen to rule the same way I was chosen. We are God's ambassadors on earth. Thy will is God's will. Thy kingdom come, thy will be done."

The servant walked to the front end of the stage and the rest of the actors froze in place. The actor read the play's original epilogue and took a bow.

The theater was silent.

The stage crew came out and lifted off the large chest plate covering Jon. He quietly followed them backstage to join the rest of the cast.

The four actors from the previous scene had changed back into the living version of their characters and they no longer had ghostly faces.

Carmen finished fastening the back of the scarlet Tudor dress that Emma wore once again. Jon thought her radiant beauty perfectly complimented her magnificent costume. All the actors looked at Jon.

"Wait for it," he said as he cupped a hand to his ear.

A moment later the theater erupted into applause. Jon grinned and belted out a hearty Henry VIII laugh. The other actors smiled and laughed as well and they began filing on stage.

The minor characters with no lines went out first, followed by those with increasingly larger roles. Everyone had gone onstage except Jon, Emma, and Carmen. The friends looked at each other and smiled.

Carmen stepped on stage and the cheering began. Emma followed a few moments later and the cheering grew louder. Jon waited a few moments and then he ran out onto the stage and circled the entire cast before he came to a stop at the front of the stage, between Emma and Carmen.

The actors held hands, smiled, and took a deep bow together. Everyone in the galleries stood to their feet and continued to applaud.

Jon looked at the faces of the audience and knew many of them had had an emotional experience. He felt that Will Shakespeare would be proud to have his original and most-provocative ending restored to its full and uncensored glory. Furthermore, Jon believed the ghost of Anne Boleyn and so many others were able to find peace.

The actors dropped hands and left the stage while the applause continued for several minutes.

Jon walked through the backstage, down the hallway and to a small but private dressing room behind a door labeled "Henry VIII," where he began to disrobe from his regalia.

He removed King Henry's oversized crown, jerkin, doublet, codpiece, and breeches. Jon wore a girdle over his undergarments as he sat in front of his lighted mirror.

He carefully removed his false beard and smeared cold cream over his face to remove his makeup and soften his skin. He wiped the cold cream off his face, brushed his hair back to his normal style, and put on his tweed suit. Jon finished tying his black necktie in front of the mirror and someone knocked on his dressing room door.

Jon answered the door and Steve came in. Steve had shaved off his beard after he and Carmen broke off their relationship earlier in the week.

"Great job tonight!" Steve said as Jon shut the door. "I've learned more about acting by watching you for the last month than I did in an entire year at theater school."

There was another knock at the door. Jon opened it.

Ryan was standing outside. Jon had not seen his friend in nearly three weeks and thought Ryan looked unusually tired and gaunt. Ryan was wearing his brown tweed suit and his beard was neatly trimmed. Jon beckoned him inside the small dressing room with Steve.

"Your King Henry will haunt my dreams," Ryan said. He handed Jon a dozen yellow roses. "You were fabulous tonight."

Jon accepted Ryan's flowers with a friendly hug.

"I'm so happy to see you, my friend," Jon said. "So much has happened. Let me introduce you to my other friend, Steve. Steve, this is Emma's brother Ryan. He helped me find that leather couch."

Ryan and Steve shook hands.

"Good to meet you, Ryan," Steve said. "I've been crashing on Jon's couch all week. My old lady kicked me out last weekend."

"Sounds like you've had a rough week," Ryan said. "The paparazzi have been stalking Emma since opening night and I think she's going crazy. There's a mob of them outside right now. All the tabloids are full of lies and rumors about her and she can't go anywhere without being recognized. I came by to see if you'd care to take a walk. I have some news of my own to share."

"It's always a pleasure," Jon said. "Steve, I'm going to go on a walk with Ryan. I'll catch up with you later."

"Can I have the keys to your flat?" Steve asked. "I'm going to crash on the couch."

Jon handed Steve his house keys.

"Thanks," Steve said. "Nice meeting you, Ryan."

Steve opened the door and Carmen was standing right outside with her hand poised to knock. She was wearing an iridescent dress with long green sleeves. Jon recognized that Carmen was beguiling him with his own fantasies. The three men stared at her.

"Oh, hi, Steve, is Jon here?" Carmen asked.

Steve and Carmen awkwardly passed each other in the doorway as Steve exited. Jon shut the door again.

"You were a wonderful tyrant tonight," Carmen said as she gave Jon a friendly hug. "I came by to see if you wanted to go out. It's Friday night, we're both single, and we don't have another show until next Wednesday."

Carmen noticed the yellow roses Jon held and she looked at Ryan.

"Unless you have made other plans," she added.

"Carmen, this is Ryan, Emma's twin brother," Jon said. "Ryan, meet Carmen."

"It's good to finally meet you," Carmen said as they shook hands. "Jon says you're old-fashioned like him. I like old-fashioned but I'm also open to new ideas."

"Maybe I should leave you two alone," Ryan said.

"No, we are going on a walk, remember?" Jon said.

"I could come with you," Carmen offered. "I could do with a good workout tonight."

"Your reputation proceeds you, milady," Ryan said. "I just met Steve. He was sad that you threw him out."

"Steve has been sleeping at my apartment all week," Jon said. "He's on his way there now."

"You're letting him stay with you?" she asked.

"He had nowhere else to go," Jon said. "I couldn't let him sleep on the streets. But he would, for you."

Carmen put her face in her hands.

"I'm sorry," she said. Carmen looked up at Jon with watery eyes. "I didn't know you were such a good friend."

"Steve speaks of you constantly. He pines for you during the day and cries out your name in his sleep."

"That sounds miserable," she said.

"It would be unbearable, but for my own pitiful state, which darkens my sun like an eclipsing moon," Jon said. "Emma cannot be replaced. She is too important to me. I thought we were perfect together, but we are missing a crucial piece."

"What's that?" Carmen asked. "If you don't mind."

"Trust," Jon said.

"You don't trust each other?" Carmen asked. "I don't think Emma was cheating on you, and I don't think Steve was cheating on me, either."

"Then why did you break up?" Jon asked.

"Steve is boring," she said. "He's so predictable and obvious. I have a competitive nature and Steve lets me win. He's fine with everything, including losing the lead role to you. It bothers me that he doesn't try harder. But I still miss him."

"You should encourage him to follow his dreams and to master his craft," Jon said. "Ask for his opinion. Support his choices. Don't put him down or deliberately undermine his confidence, or your man may become a shadow of his former self."

"You're right, Jon," Carmen said. "I have been too hard on Steve lately. He's a good man."

"And a loyal friend," Jon added.

"A loyal boyfriend, too," Carmen said. "Can I talk to

him? I need to see him again."

Jon told Carmen his address and she thanked him.

"It was good to finally meet you," Carmen said to Ryan, then she addressed Jon. "I hope you and Emma find that missing piece. You two belong together."

Jon and Ryan went out the front door together, past hundreds of people waiting for the chance to see the starring actors. Jon was unrecognizable as Henry VIII without his false beard. The fans recognized Carmen and showered her with adoration and praise.

Jon and Ryan walked together until they were clear of the crowds and found a quiet place to talk.

"What is your news?" Jon asked.

"I got a promotion at work," Ryan said.

"Congratulations," Jon said. "You deserve it."

"My new job is in Oxford," Ryan said.

"You're moving to Oxford? When?"

"Next week," Ryan said.

"Do you need help moving?" Jon asked. "You helped me move. I owe you a favor. It's the least I can do."

"Thank you. I will let you know if I do," Ryan said.

"Is Emma moving with you?" Jon asked.

"No, Emma needs to stay here and be a star," he said.

"Did she tell you what happened?" Jon asked.

"Not everything, but she told me you two are taking a break," Ryan said.

"Did she say why?"

"She said she was concerned about your memory."

"My memory is fine," Jon said. "I can remember everything. I remember a month ago when we first met, you said you weren't ready to move back home and settle down. A lot can happen in a month."

"Indeed, it can," Ryan said. "You found a roommate."

"Do you think Emma still loves me?" Jon asked.

Ryan's eyes began to well with tears.

"I know she still does," Ryan said. "I don't know what to tell you. Not everything that breaks can be fixed."

"Thank you for giving me hope," Jon said.

"I don't know when I will see you again, and I wanted to thank you for teaching me about what it means to be a gentleman," Ryan said. "I thought I knew, but now I see I had no idea. You have opened my eyes."

"I'm sorry that things are rough with your sister and me, and I truly hope my relationship with her has not jeopardized our friendship," Jon said. "You are both dear friends to me in different ways, and I wish I could have you both together. If only you were not a man, you might be my ideal woman."

"If I was a woman, I would be Emma, and she would be me," Ryan said. "Why didn't you go with Carmen after the play? Emma doesn't have to know everything we do. I would have kept your secret."

"I can't give Carmen what she wants because it's not what I want," Jon said. "Emma holds the key to my heart."

"You really do love Emma," Ryan said with a smile.

"I have a true secret to confide with you, but first you must promise not to tell a soul, not even our dear Emma."

"I promise," Ryan pledged.

"Swear it!" Jon commanded.

Ryan held up his right hand as a solemn oath.

"I swear I will carry your secret to my grave," he said.

"I gave the Tudor dress to Emma," Jon said.

"Actually, I think she said her friend Anne lent it to her," Ryan corrected.

"That was me," Jon said. "I gave her my dress, my bodice, and my farthingale. It really did belong to the court of Henry VIII. The shoes were hers."

"How did you get the dress?" Ryan asked.

"That dress was the only clothing I had," Jon said. "When I met Emma, I knew Anne wanted her to have it."

A large white van turned around a corner and began speeding towards them. The driver of the van was typing a message to someone on a smartphone and was not paying attention to the road.

"You saw her get the dress and now you're probably confused about who gave it to her," Ryan said. "Emma said you can reassemble facts in your head to maintain and reinforce your own narrative fantasy. I can see why you are drawn to Shakespeare."

"I never told Emma because I don't want her to know it was me," Jon said. "It's too embarrassing."

"Well, your secret is safe with me," Ryan said.

"You promise you won't tell anyone?" Jon asked.

"No one would believe me. Not even Emma."

The driver of the speeding van received a message that caused them to fly into a rage upon reading it. They furiously texted back a reply while continuing to drive.

"You're a true friend, Ryan, and I'm glad to know you," Jon said. "I love you like a brother."

"I love you too," Ryan said. He gave Jon a tight hug.

"You take care of yourself."

Ryan watched as Jon turned away and stepped out into the street, directly into the path of the oncoming van. Ryan saw the van at the last minute.

"Jon! Look out!" he yelled.

Jon looked back at his friend and found himself being tackled to the ground just as the speeding white van tore past. Jon heard a loud thump and the van's brakes screeched the vehicle to a halt.

Ryan screamed out in agony.

Jon stood up and realized he was not hurt. Ryan was lying on the pavement in the middle of the road, clutching his right leg, and crying out in pain. The yellow roses were scattered all over the street.

The driver of the van ran over to Jon and Ryan.

"Please call for help!" Jon said.

The van's driver took out a smartphone and dialed the number for emergencies.

Jon looked at Ryan's injured leg closer and saw it was clearly bent in the wrong direction. There was no blood.

"You saved my life!" Jon cried as he tried to comfort his injured friend.

"This is going to ruin my plans," Ryan said just before he lost consciousness.

The driver of the van recited a prayer for Ryan and arranged the yellow roses to encircle him. An ambulance and a police car arrived a few minutes later. The paramedics rushed over to help Ryan.

Jon explained what happened to the police while Ryan was put onto a stretcher and loaded into the back of the ambulance. The driver of the van was placed in police custody in the back seat of the patrol car until authorities could determine the extent of Ryan's injuries.

"Where are you taking my friend?" Jon asked one of the paramedics before they left.

"London Bridge Hospital," they said as they closed the back doors of the ambulance. Bright lights and sirens erupted from the ambulance as it sped eastward in the direction of the hospital.

Jon asked the police officer if he could get a ride to the hospital but such a favor was not allowed. The police said they had to stay with the suspect and the vehicle.

Jon tried to hail a taxi but had no luck. He looked around for a landmark and saw the glowing spire of the Shard skyscraper in the distance. He knew the hospital was north of the Shard and began to run in its direction.

He thought of his friend as he ran. Jon remembered the time he and Ryan raced to the leather couch they found on a street corner. He remembered Ryan helped him carry that couch up four flights of stairs to the apartment Ryan helped him find.

Jon thought he should try to find Emma and tell her about Ryan, but he had not seen Emma outside of work all week. Hardly anyone had. After opening night, it seemed everyone was talking about the new ending to Henry VIII. The story was in all the tabloid newspapers, along with gossip about the actors' bizarre personal habits.

Jon decided he would try to notify Emma when he got to the hospital. He didn't have a phone, but he remembered her phone number.

He was mindful about cross traffic at intersections and continued running until he arrived, breathless, at the hospital reception area. It took Jon half a minute to catch his breath.

"Hi, I'm looking for my friend," he said. "His name is Ryan Morgan. He was just in an accident. We were both just in an accident. Ryan broke his leg saving my life. I ran all the way here."

The nurse looked at her computer screen, frowned, and then tapped a few buttons on her keyboard.

"Did you say Ryan Morgan?" she asked. "We don't have any patients here by that name. What is your name?"

"My name is Jon Henry."

"How are you related to Mr. Morgan?"

"I owest him my life!" Jon said. "He broke his leg and an ambulance brought him here not twenty minutes ago. We are best friends."

Jon read the nurse's name tag. Her name was Helen.

"We did have a broken leg come in about fifteen minutes ago," she said as she checked her computer screen again. "They are currently in surgery. I was here when this patient came in. I recall there was a bit of a mix-up at check-in."

"A mix-up?" Jon asked. He had heard that expression before.

"It's uncommon, but we had a similar situation here about a month ago," Nurse Helen said. She looked up from her monitor and took a closer look at Jon's face. "Ophelia? O.M.G.! I can't believe it's you!"

She stood up and ran around the desk to the front and

gave Jon a hug. She wore green hospital scrubs and rubber clogs that muffled the sound of her footsteps.

Jon remembered his favorite nurse again and returned the embrace. He recalled walking laps around these brightly lit hospital corridors for hours every day while he was recovering his strength. He used to chat with the people he saw during his walks and now their faces became more familiar to him. Jon recognized he had returned to the place where he began his new life.

"I remember this place," Jon said to the twenty or so people gathered around him in the hallway. "You all saved me. I thank you again."

"How have you been?" Helen asked.

"Most excellent," he said. "I have a job, a home, and a girlfriend, and I'm surrounded by good friends. My best friend is in here with a broken leg he got by saving me. I owe him my life."

Once he had caught up with the crowd about the past month, Jon found a payphone and made his first telephone call. He put some coins in the money slot and dialed the number to Emma's smartphone. He held the receiver to his ear like he had seen others do. The call rang through four clicks before it played a recording of Emma's voice.

"Hi, you've reached Emma's phone. Leave a message and Emma will call you back. Thanks!"

"Hi Emma, it's Jon …"

An unfamiliar voice interrupted: "The recipient's mailbox is full. Goodbye!"

The call disconnected and Jon heard a dial tone. He hung up the receiver and did not receive a refund. He sat down frustrated in a nearby chair and waited. There were several daily newspapers on the table next to him.

Jon didn't typically read the tabloids but he was fascinated to see pictures of himself in print next to stories about *Henry VIII* in which he was quoted. The media loved Emma most of all, and they showed it by publishing old photos of her with her ex-husband next to scandalous articles about her alleged promiscuity, all attributed to anonymous sources.

He traded the tabloid for a leather-bound copy of the *King James Version*. Jon turned to the end and began to read the Revelation of St. John. As he read the words, Jon felt transported back to St. Saviour's Church in 1613.

"I am Alpha and Omega, the beginning and the ending," Jon read, and imagined Will's voice speaking the words of the spirit. "I am he that liveth and was dead; and behold, I am alive for evermore, Amen."

Half an hour passed before someone told Jon he could visit his friend. They walked with him down the familiar hallways and showed him to the room. Jon went inside.

He was confused to discover Emma lying on the hospital bed with a cast on her right leg. She wore a blue gown, just as Jon had worn when he was a patient. He felt a rush of emotions pour over him at once and suddenly everything became clear.

"Hey, Shakespeare," she said weakly.

"What happened to you?"

"You could call it providence," Emma said. "I barely remember it happening. There wasn't time to think. I saw the van and just reacted."

"You saved me?" he asked, trying to believe it.

"You would have saved me if you had seen it first," she said. "I couldn't lose you. I had to."

Jon rushed to Emma's bedside and showered her with kisses of gratitude, love, and admiration.

"I'm so sorry I lied to you," she said. "I don't have a brother. It started as a lark because I thought you were a pompous phony, and a little crazy, but then I got to know you better and realized you're actually incredible. You are the man of my dreams. I wanted to tell you the truth so many times but I didn't know how. I feel like such a fool."

The emergency room doctor came in and Jon recognized him.

"Dr. Fuchsia," Jon said, and he extended his hand. "Jon Henry."

"You were here a month ago, weren't you?" the doctor asked as he shook Jon's hand. "You look healthy. How are you feeling?"

"I feel great, and I think I'm adjusting well, but I'm still confused about my past and so many things still don't make sense," Jon said.

"Have you been drinking alcohol?" he asked.

"Not a drop, doc," Jon said. "I've been good."

"I can attest to Jon's sobriety," Emma said.

"That's wonderful," Fuchsia said. "It's always a treat to see my patients after they've recovered. How well do you know Emma?"

"We work together," Jon said. "She's my girlfriend and also my best friend. She's the love of my life."

"That's terrific," Dr. Fuchsia said. "Can I share a

story with Emma about your medical history?"

"You can tell her anything," Jon said. "We don't have any more secrets."

"I'm really happy for you two," Fuchsia said. "It's ironic that she came in here dressed as a man, because you came in here dressed as a woman. I remember it was a gorgeous scarlet dress, in the Tudor Renaissance style if I'm not mistaken."

"Anne?" Emma asked. "That was really you?"

"I had to wear it just once because I was desperate, and you were so kind to me," Jon said. "Thank you again, and I'm sorry I couldn't tell you."

Jon and Emma held hands and gazed into each other's eyes. Jon knew they would find a way to fix this.

"When Jon first came in here, he was cold as ice, in a coma, and he had severe alcohol poisoning, but he still had a faint pulse," Dr. Fuchsia continued. "We didn't know if you would survive, but when you warmed up, you sobered up. After you regained consciousness, you listed your emergency contact as William Shakespeare! You were fine, medically, so we released you. I'm very pleased with your recovery."

"Thank you, doctor," Jon said.

"You're a lot older than you look," Emma said.

Dr. Fuchsia checked his clipboard and addressed Emma next.

"Try to rest your leg and use crutches or a wheelchair to keep weight off it for two months," Fuchsia said. "You're not pregnant, but you're a little malnourished and you should try to eat healthier so your leg heals properly.

You will need to schedule an appointment for x-rays in a week, and I will write you a prescription for pain pills. You can take her home now, Jon."

The doctor left the room. Jon and Emma looked at each other lovingly.

"Now you know all my secrets," Jon said.

"And you know all mine," Emma said. "We've already been friends and lovers. Maybe we can make it work this time."

Nurse Helen arrived at the door with a wheelchair and the brown tweed suit.

Jon and Helen both helped Emma get out of bed and into the wheelchair. Her cast hung out in front.

Jon pushed Emma's chair down the winding hallways toward the main entrance.

"Does Steve know what we did on the couch?" Emma asked.

"Ha!" Jon laughed. "Don't tell him; he loves that couch. I just remembered Carmen went to my apartment. Do you think they're testing out the couch?"

"I don't think I will make it up your stairs for at least a month," Emma said. "Let's go back to my place."

Jon and Emma exited the hospital through the main sliding-glass doors, and they were immediately swarmed by paparazzi with flashing cameras and hundreds of adoring fans.

The end.

About the Author

Jake Blake is a novelist from Toledo, Washington. He holds a Master of Arts degree from Washington State University. This is his third published novel.

In 2016, Jake was trampled by a runaway horse and carriage while attending a fair. He saved his four-year-old child, but suffered a traumatic brain injury and spent a month in the hospital before returning to recover in provincial Toledo. Writing became a form of therapy. His Providence got a cat.

When his brain recovered, Jake imagined a character frozen in their time and reawakened in our time. Jake selected the 1613 Globe Theater fire as the setting and this story unfolded. Henry VIII likely suffered a traumatic brain injury during a horse accident.

William Shakespeare's inspiration on this novel has lifted *Shakespeare On Ice* to a higher dimension. The time dedicated to researching his genius has been joyous, and the Tudor family gossip will always feel fresh and juicy.

Suggested Reading

Beckett, Samuel. *Waiting for Godot: A Tragicomedy in Two Acts*. Grove Press, 2011. Written in 1954.

Bryson, Bill. *Shakespeare: The World as Stage*. Harper Perennial, 2009.

De Lisle, Leanda. *After Elizabeth: The Rise of King James of Scotland and the Struggle for the Throne of England*. Ballantine Books, 2007.

Edelstein, Barry. *Thinking Shakespeare: A Working Guide for Actors, Directors, Students... and Anyone Else Interested in the Bard*. Spark Publishing, 2007.

Edmondson, Paul. *Shakespeare: An Introduction: Ideas in Profile*. Profile Books Ltd, 2015.

Garber, Marjorie. *Shakespeare and Modern Culture*. Pantheon Books, 2008.

Greenblatt, Stephen. *Tyrant: Shakespeare on Politics*. W. W. Norton & Company, 2018.

Greenblatt, Stephen. *Will in the World: How Shakespeare Became Shakespeare*. W. W. Norton & Company, 2004.

Greer, Germain. *Shakespeare's Wife*. Harper Perennial, 2007.

Huxley, Aldous. *Brave New World*. HarperCollins, Harper Perennial, 1932.

King James Version. Holy Bible. First published in 1611.

Kafka, Franz. *Metamorphosis*. Bantam Classics, 1972.

King, Stephen. *On Writing: A Memoir of the Craft*. Scribner, 2000.

Marche, Stephen. *How Shakespeare Changed Everything*. Harper Perennial, 2012.

Norton, David. *The King James Bible: A Short History from Tyndale to Today*. Cambridge University Press, 2011.

Picard, Liza. *Elizabeth's London: Everyday life in Elizabethan London*. St. Martin's Press, 2004.

Rosenbaum, Ron. *The Shakespeare Wars: Clashing Scholars, Public Fiascoes, Palace Coups*. Random House, 2006.

Singman, Jeffrey. *Daily Life in Elizabethan England*. Greenwood Press, 1995.

Shakespeare, William. *The Complete Works of William Shakespeare*. First published in 1623.

Shapiro, James. *Contested Will: Who Wrote Shakespeare?* Simon & Schuster, 2011.

Stoppard, Tom. *Rosencrantz & Guildenstern are Dead*. Grove Press, 2017. Written in 1967.

Wells, Stanley. *The Shakespeare Book: Big Ideas Simply Explained*. DK, 2019.

If you enjoyed this book, share it with a friend.

Made in the USA
Middletown, DE
15 November 2020